FORBIDDEN FRUIT

ALSO BY KIMBERLEY M. BYRD

Son of the Forgiven (Book 2)

Vengeance Is Mine (Book 3, Coming Soon)

NON-FICTION

10 Commandments for Dream Chaser

For more information visit

www.WriteOnKim.com

FORBIDDEN FRUIT

KIMBERLEY M. BYRD

Ward Eternal
PUBLISHING

Forbidden Fruit

a novel by

Kimberley M. Byrd

Word Eternal, Inc.

P.O. Box 625

Troy, AL 36081

Copyright © 2015 by Kimberley M. Byrd

ISBN: 978-0-9794433-2-9

Author's photo by B M Photography

Cover Design by Word Eternal, Inc.

Cover Photo by D. Pham

Printed in the United States of America

In Memory of

Pastelene McClure

March 18, 1936 – October 2, 2005

This book is dedicated to the memory of my beautiful mother, Pastelene Jones-McClure, who has soared home to be with the Lord. I miss you severely and love you dearly. Thank you so much for everything that you have placed into me and believed that I could be.

Gracious Mother, we release you.

<u>In The Beginning</u> 1

K enali King felt as if she was inside of herself; breathing amplified, heart beating between her ears. Her senses were on high alert confusing her even more since the tears stubbornly refused to come.

It could not be that her heart was hardened; she heard it shatter a few seconds ago. Neither could it be that she was emotionless. She had cried many times before in her thirty-one years on this earth. Yet, when it counted the most; nothing.

Even replaying repeatedly how everything here at the hospital unfolded. First, it was a nurse coming into the waiting room to give her an unprofessional, frantic update.

"Oh, my God! They're working on her," pausing to breathe heavily with her hand on her chest. "Her heart stopped. They're trying to revive her. I'm so sorry. I'll be praying for you."

The teary-eyed countenance of this nurse was shocking for as far as Kenali knew she was a total stranger. Then again, her mother had been to this hospital many times since her kidneys failed a few years back. Yet each time she would always come home. Today coming home was being threatened according to the recent news of the nurse. When people say they will pray, that is normally a reference to how bad things really are.

A few minutes later, the ultimate blow was dealt; the doctor coming himself. After many times of amusing at his bubbly character, which her mother just loved about him, Kenali just shook her head to prepare for the painful words which his actions relayed he was about to deliver. She absentmindedly sucked her teeth.

The painful words he must have prepared on his way down the hall were wretched to her ears.

"Kenali," he paused, "the complications with your mother's kidneys just took a toll on her body over the years. It was just too much on her heart. I'm sorry, Kenali, but there was nothing more we could do. I'm sorry." He rubbed her arm gently.

I know something you can do. You can march back into that room as fast as those soft bottom shoes can carry you and bring my mama back to life.

Her thoughts were more demanding than she was.

After she didn't say anything, the doctor asked, "Where's Mr. King?"

"He and Divine are on the way." Her words were robotic in nature. Kenali never moved. Never blinked.

They should have been here by now. Why am I getting this news alone? I wonder what mama cooked for our lunch date that I blew off so that I could finish writing. I'm so selfish. Oh, my God, my mama is gone.

Her tormenting thoughts were all over the place.

Now minutes later after receiving the most horrific news known to her, she was still numb. She had heard that before people died, their life would flash before their eyes but they never said the same was true for the survivors. Every event she and her mom shared was flashing before her eyes that stubbornly held back the tears.

This entire ordeal just felt so indescribably out of order that her emotions even exceeded description. Everything on the countertop of the hospital was so neatly ordered that

2

she wanted to disrupt it so it would mimic her right now. The clock on the wall thundered as the second hand's ticking became a thong. The whiteness of the walls was as blinding as snow for miles without interruption. The absence of the beeps from the machines here at her mother's bedside haunted her as the silence represented death.

Replaying their conversation from this morning, her mother was just fine. Even over the phone, her sparkling personality arose to meet Kenali's ears. She was just as uniquely beautiful as her name Pastoria which was given to her by an Indian friend of her mother.

Kenali began to rub the silver and black strands of her mother's hair. The majority of the silver naturally congregated slightly off center of the front of her head. It gave her the appearance of an eccentric performer or a superhero. The silver patch was the focal point of her beautiful face.

She had never seen her this lifeless before. She looked like she was sleeping beauty taking a nap. Her flesh was still warm. Her hands were still the same.

Kenali exhaled loudly rubbing her hands down the sides of her face to clasp over her mouth.

Just because I don't cry won't make the truth change. Deep on the inside, she was refusing to accept it. She was so accustomed to believing things could change for the positive. *Why couldn't the nurse have come to tell me to pray sooner? Why wasn't I already praying?*

Kenali knew the value and power of prayer. It was because she had been released from some things that she shouldn't have survived. She had transitioned from writing erotica to writing inspirational novels along with self-help books, which evolved her into a motivational speaker. However, regardless of how positive she was, nothing could be done here.

Divine, her oldest sister and their dad, Alto King came bursting through the door, shaking her from her thoughts. The unreadable look she expressed confused them. However, when Divine focused on their mother she let out a blood-curdling scream.

"Mama!" Divine covered her mouth. "Mama is gone." Divine almost dove on top of her mother with an embrace which for the first time ever wasn't returned.

Don't say that Divine!

Kenali's lips parted but nothing came out but the long awaited tears. Having heard Divine say it and watching her daddy's expression of grief made it all real. There was nothing she could do about it.

"Pastoria? Honey?" He patted his beloved wife's hand as if to wake her from a nap.

"Daddy, she's gone." Kenali's words trembled past her lips as she broke down into the arms of her daddy.

Divine continued to press her ear to their mama's chest as if to see if some horrible lie had been told. She kept repeating the same words in varying octaves. "My mama? My mama! Oh my mama!"

Kenali was now free to cry but since she held it in so long, she collapsed.

While blacked out, she thought of her mama prepping a meal humming as she sashayed around the kitchen just as she had always done. She had on an apron inscribed with "Give God a Praise at All Times" which was the epitome of the life her mama lived. Then her mama stopped humming, looking at her giving her some motherly encouragement.

"Baby girl, it's alright. Count it all joy."

Then she faded away.

"Baby girl. Baby girl. Wake up," she heard her daddy saying the more she came too.

He had those big tears in his eyes; the kind that hadn't streamed yet but puddled. Then one launched hitting her in the face.

This was a bad day, she thought. Three things that never happened before just did. One, she had never fainted. Two, she had never seen her dad cry. And three, which was the total worst, her mama had never died. There was no way that she could ever count this as being a part of joy.

GOD CREATED 2

When Kenali woke up in her childhood bedroom, she looked around with familiar confusion. The more she awakened, the more she hurt all over again. Everyday was the same fresh batch of pain in which she had to remember the tragedy of what had transpired only a couple of days ago.

Her head was pounding to the point she thought her brain wanted to jump out her skull. She felt so heavy. This feeling was for the reason of she hadn't really slept a wink since the day at the hospital. All night long, she attempted to mentally prepare herself for the swiftly approaching funeral.

Throwing her legs over the side of the bed, she supported the overwhelming weight of her head with her hands. She squinted due to the much too bright sunlight peering through the window. Ordinarily she enjoyed a beautifully sunlit day. However, the pounding headache that was ransacking her head prevented her from doing so today.

Instead of a lack of sleep, this felt like the one and only hangover that she had experienced during the time when she and her then boyfriend were having relationship problems. She somehow felt that she could just drink until it all went away but she was painfully wrong. One good thing came out of that overconsumption; she never wanted to take another drink.

"Oh, God, my head is killing me," she whispered.

Forcing herself to get up since the urge to use the restroom was getting stronger by the second. She walked like a blind person who had lost their cane. Holding one hand extended in front of her, she grabbed anything that could assist her journey to the toilet. There was a queasy feeling in the pit of her stomach, which made the headache even worse. She walked carefully.

"I think Simbol spiked my orange juice," Kenali groggily spoke. She became reintroduced to the slickness of her sister that in birth order was between Kenali and Divine. Being devilish had always been a part of her character. She proved last night that it will always be.

Finally making it to the toilet thanks to the aide of chairs and walls, she sat there in a slump. Her body was so limp even her head just hung backwards as far as her neck would allow. Being that her mouth was already lazily open, she sighed deeply at the thought of having to move again.

Kenali dragged her feet until she got to the sink washing her hands with her elbows on the counter. She caught a glimpse of herself that made her look twice. Her reddened puffy eyes had dark circles underneath them and her skin looked dull. Rubbing her cold water dampened hands onto her face, Kenali hoped that these not so beautiful flaws would somehow just rub off returning her skin back to its normal vibrancy. It did not but the coolness of the water sure felt good to her skin.

Yeah. Simbol got me good.

She then bent over the sink to splash handfuls of cold crisp water onto her face. The refreshing nature of it seemed to calm her headache a great bit.

While she put a moisturizer on her face, she began to notice how much she actually looked like her mom. They had the same hairline which came to a point in the middle of their foreheads. Even the pecan shape of Kenali's eyes minus the puffiness was like her mother's. Not being able to resist, she lightly traced them with her fingertips.

Looking at her reflection, her eyes filled with tears. Seemingly, out of her control, her face cringed as if she wanted to yell but stay silent at the same time. She braced herself on the countertop with both hands. Her shoulders shrugged upward and she slowly lowered her head to lay in the locks of them. The same tears that refused to come in the beginning now could find no end as they fell into the sink of water making small ripples.

After she heard a knock on the bedroom door, she almost wanted to hide the fact she was crying. However, she continued silently, thinking whoever was knocking wouldn't see her in the bed and just leave. She was wrong. She felt a presence at the entrance to the bathroom. Thankfully, she had closed the door.

Simbol's voice ladened with concern came from outside the door.

"Kenali, are you ok?"

Yeah, I'm ok. Mom just died. That's all. Kenali refrained from what she wanted to say being that it was riddled with sarcasm.

"I'll be ok," she managed to say under a muffled breath. Kenali inhaled deeply to get herself together.

She knew all too well if Simbol saw her crying then she was going to join in—dramatically. Kenali had no clue how Simbol was going to make it through the funeral. Everybody knew that it was going to be a problem for her. That's part of the reason why their dad didn't tell her what had happened over the phone until a relative was in Atlanta on Simbol's doorstep.

Kenali always contributed Simbol's dual personality to her being the second daughter. Dependent upon who you were to her, would determine which one you would receive; the super tough or the super softhearted cry baby. Simbol always thought of herself normal while Kenali was adamant about affixing the label of bipolar onto her.

"Daddy wants to talk to the three of us downstairs in a few minutes," Simbol spoke pressing her ear to the door.

After a brief moment, Kenali responded. "Ok. Be right down."

"Do you want me to wait for you?"

Something on the inside of Kenali was saying, "No," however, she did want some company. When she rushed to open the door, Simbol almost fell inside the bathroom but attempted to play it off.

"Whoa! I didn't know you were on the door," Kenali explained.

"What are you talking about? I just thought you needed a hug."

Pulling back from the cover up hug, Simbol looked into Kenali's face. Her complete tone of voice turned extremely sympathetic.

"Oh, Kenali, you look a mess. You were crying weren't you? I'm sorry."

Noticing the tears welling up in Simbol's eyes, Kenali had to deflect it somehow.

"You should be sorry for spiking my drink last night."

Simbol gave a sheepish grin despite the already forming tears looming in her eyes threatening to fall.

"You needed it. I was trying to help you sleep."

"Yeah, right." She smiled as much as her headache would allow. "So what does Dad want to talk to us about?"

Simbol blinked repeatedly. "I don't know. Let's go find out."

Both pajama-wearing sisters wrapped their arms around each other and began to walk down the stairs where they met Divine.

"Hey, girls," Divine sounded so much like their mom.

"Hey, big sis." Kenali hugged Divine in greeting.

"Where's daddy?" Simbol asked.

"He went outside onto the porch," Divine replied looking in the direction of the French doors.

"I've never seen him this sad before. He's probably having a hard time when he sleeps with mom's side of the bed being empty and all," Simbol remarked with an excruciatingly saddened look on her face.

"Yeah, it has to be extra hard for him. Forty-eight years and no longer than a weekend apart," Kenali expressed.

"So what are we going to do about Dad being in this big house all by himself?" Simbol questioned looking back towards the stairs she recently descended.

She could remember running up those stairs when they first moved in. Her mother always cautioned her to be careful although she gently ignored it to explore every inch of their new house. It was just as she had said—big. When compared with the tiny two-bedroom house they had moved from, this was a mansion in which there were no more room sharing. Divine made those funny noises with her throat while she was asleep. And there was no way she was going to share with her new baby sister.

Now Simbol wondered how she could be a part of the solution with her living three hours away in Atlanta.

"Divine and I live close by," Kenali suggested.

"But don't you think he'll be lonely in here all alone?" Simbol just couldn't get used to the idea.

"Since Divine has a family it wouldn't be fair to Gerald and the boys for her to uproot. So that leaves me to move in with him for a while until things ease up." Kenali

paused to think. "And you don't have anybody either, so it would be easy for you to just pick up and come back to town for a while as well," Kenali replied.

Simbol was slightly offended. "What do you mean I don't have anybody? How do you know what's going on in my love life?"

"I didn't mean it like—"

"Whatever," Simbol said with a slight smile on her face.

"Divine, what are you going to do with *your* sister," Kenali emphasized ownership.

"Nothing. After dealing with her as long as I have, I know better. Some things with Simbol you just learn to leave alone," Divine giggled while she was talking.

"This sounds like a double team. I'm going to go out there with *my* daddy."

Simbol spoke in a spoiled little girl tone, with being forty, she was much too old to possess. Then she threw her nose in the air and walked away.

Divine and Kenali looked at each other shaking their heads laughing as Simbol exited the French doors to the porch.

"She never did get over you replacing her as the baby girl," Divine laughed. "Let's go out there with Dad. We need the fresh air anyway. Especially you. Got a hangover?"

"Simbol."

"Say no more. I've known her longer." Divine laughed shaking her head.

The two sisters walked outside to join their dad and a spoiled rotten Simbol who had already positioned herself in the rocking chair closest to him. It was their mom's designated seat by choice.

He looked their way as they came through the doors. His rhythm of rocking was soothing to watch for some reason. Kenali almost mimicked the motion while she was standing leaning against the wall. Divine stretched out on the chaise lounge.

Everywhere Kenali looked was surrounded by a memory of her mom. They had so many cookouts and conversations on this porch and backyard over the 31 years they lived here.

It was under the white petal covered Bradford Pear tree that her mom told her the story of this house being built right before Kenali was born. People called them wannabe big shots because as a couple they wanted more for their growing family. From that day on, her dad's name, Alto King, became associated with money. That in itself attracted a specific type of crowd to come feeling entitled to a piece of his hard earned money.

Although he never entertained the talkers with an answer, in his heart he knew that he had to teach his children the important life lessons of making an honest living and of how a real man is supposed to provide for his family. In every decision, Kenali could always remember her mom quietly supporting her dad.

This is going to be very hard. All of these memories are flooding me.

Kenali had her worst break down the first day that she woke up in her old bedroom. She spotted a doll her mom had gotten her so long ago on her sixteenth birthday. It was a porcelain doll with a hand crocheted red and white antebellum dress, with a matching hat and purse. Just the sight of the doll caused not only her tears to flood but also the memory of the day she received it.

"Kenali, I have a surprise for you," Pastoria chimed with a melody to her words.

Kenali's curiosity stood at attention.

"What is it, Mama?" A freshly turned 16-year old Kenali asked with brightened eyes.

"Do you want to guess what it is or do you want me to tell you?"

"Telling me makes it faster."

Kenali hoped that her mom would cut to the chase. After all, it was her birthday and the suspense was killing her.

"I shouldn't have said anything. I want you to open it this afternoon at your birthday party. Just forget that I said anything."

Her mama toyed with her by walking away with a large box in her hand.

I wonder what the penalty of grabbing the box and running would be.

"Mama, please don't torture me like this. Please. I'll wash the dishes for a week."

"Are you trying to pull a fast one on me? You already wash the dishes anyway."

"Oh, yeah. I keep forgetting that since I was born soooooo much later that I'm the only one left here. I guess it's the suffering that I have to endure for being a mistake," Kenali sadly proclaimed with a very effective face to match.

"Here, baby. You were not a mistake. You just came a little later...and unexpectedly. That's all. But never a mistake."

Pastoria's heart softened toward her child. She ended toying with Kenali to hand the box over.

Checkmate, Kenali thought. Her technique worked like a charm. However, that tactic couldn't be used again for a few months.

As Kenali began to tear into the box, she sized it up trying to figure out what was in it. Was it something disguised in a huge box that would serve as a hint she was getting a car?

The tape was a hindrance to her. She finally made it through all the wrapping. When she had removed everything and looked down into the box, Kenali's face showed bewilderment.

"A doll?" Kenali was discombobulated.

Kenali shook the doll to see if any keys would fall from under its dress.

Kenali's disappointment was on target with Pastoria's expectancy.

"Kenali, you're growing up so fast becoming a beautiful young lady. One day you'll get married to a wonderful man who loves you and you'll have children." Pastoria winked at Kenali squeezing her shoulders. "When I looked down into your crib, I saw a one of a kind original lying there. Just like my other girls, you were different in your own way. This doll represents you and hopefully one day you will give it to your daughter to let her know that she's an original. And make sure the man that you marry treats you the same way."

After her mother stopped speaking, Kenali thought for a moment before her face paraded felicity. She grabbed her mother and they laughed together in a warm embrace making that birthday the best one ever even before she got the keys to her new car.

Now, on the porch, Kenali pressed her back into the wall hard to suppress the tears she felt swelling up on the inside. She grieved over the fact she had missed their last lunch together. She toiled over knowing that she wasn't even praying at the hospital. Before she could further abuse herself, her daddy's voice cut into her thoughts.

"Girls, I just want the three of you to know that this is going to be a trying time for us all. And I want you to brace yourselves for the funeral tomorrow. I know what it's like to lose a mother. It hurts," he paused.

Thinking to himself how he has never lost a wife before, he swallowed hard. He needed to find a way to apply his own advice so he could be strong for his daughters.

The four of them had an unannounced moment of silence with each of them fighting back tears. There was sniffing and the clearing of throats that needed no explanation. Simbol cried the hardest.

"You know your mother would have wanted you girls to be strong. She was so graceful. So no falling out at the funeral, Simbol," he slyly added.

"Ok, Daddy. I'm going to try my best."

Simbol was no weakling. She just couldn't handle sad occasions and everyone knew it.

"Dad, we were talking about keeping a check on you for the next few weeks. Kenali said that she could stay here for as long as you needed her," Divine added.

She intended to take some of the tension out of the conversation about the funeral but this didn't seem to be the right way to do so. It brought even more awareness to their mother's absence.

Their dad shook his head while biting on his bottom lip.

"I sure would appreciate that. I don't want to inconvenience anybody but just for a little while would be good."

"Daddy, that's not an inconvenience. I would be glad to." Kenali placed her hand on her daddy's shoulder very close to his neck. When he began speaking again, she felt the vibration of the bass in his voice.

"I was thinking about that last night. Being in this big house all by myself. Never wanted to see this day."

He stared without blinking out into the distance of green grass and trees. His eyes travelled as far as he could see although he had no intended focal point. However, it was soothing.

Kenali sat thinking back to the conversation that they had with their dad yesterday. She focused in on the part about her mom being a woman of grace. She was indeed that. She was a praying woman who had prayed her family through many things as well as taught them how to pray.

Thinking about her mother's prayer life brought more guilt upon her heart. *I knew better than to be sitting at the hospital idle. Why wasn't I praying anyway?* Her thoughts pounded her to a pulp so much she forced a shifting in them to be more about who her mother was.

There were certain of her mom's traits that she passed along to her daughters. Being delightfully pleasant and compassionate towards others was given to Divine. When she was growing up and even recently, Kenali watched how people enjoyed being around her mom. Simply, she had a heart of gold.

With being so nice, she was strong in a graceful way. There have been times in which people thought she was naïve until two weeks later when they figured out that she had gotten them told. Simbol and Kenali both possessed this trait and operated in it well. Kenali giggled inwardly.

Someone saying that it was time to go to the funeral broke Kenali's thoughts. She hated funerals. They were such an in your face reminder that it's over. Death or anything sad just wasn't a part of her inner wiring even though she understood its inevitability.

Outside of being sad, her uncle's funeral a few years ago was almost like a comical soap opera. There was drama and laughter in which everyone held out of respect.

The main event surrounded this mysterious woman drenched from head to toe in bright red. She was a bit big boned and flamboyant for lack of a better term. The family could not figure out why she was mourning so hard and openly. Her cries were disturbingly deep as her voice had a little too much bass for a woman.

This woman was some character that screamed to receive the attention of everyone by continuously wailing so dramatically loud the ushers had to escort her out of the church. The surviving wife and children could not mourn properly. They were wondering who this floozy was that had the gall to come to the funeral to show that she apparently had some form of relationship with a married man.

After a few minutes went by, the woman who had regained her composure came as quietly as her bright dress would allow, tiptoeing to the front. She sat right down by the grieving yet confused widow. It seemed as if she was trying to tell her something. But before she could get it out, the youngest daughter went to her mother's aide slapping the woman right out of the seat.

Well, the woman was on the floor looking so terrified she forgot the proper etiquette for wearing a dress. Her legs were cocked wide open with her dress up just enough to reveal herself or more like himself. When everybody caught a glimpse of his package and realized that this was a man, the whole crowd leaned back with a unison, "Whoa!"

Now the daughter was enraged from embarrassment. She dove onto the floor atop this person snatching his wig off while he snatched hers off in defense. The whole time the daughter was brawling with him, he was trying to say something and defend himself without knocking the crap out of her, as he knew he could.

Order finally came when the brother grabbed his vigilante sister around the waist with her legs and arms flailing wildly in the air. The female imposter grabbed his wig, placed it haphazardly on his head, and said that he was sorry for the mistake of coming to the funeral. He told them that he was at the wrong person's funeral. Further, he explained something about a surgical procedure on his eyes to explain that he could not see properly. With this explanation, the entire audience exhaled with a great big, "Whew," to know that their loved one was not mixed up in some extracurricular activity that included a bold big boned mistress that was actually a man.

Of course, since it was so tempting, Kenali wrote that scene into one of her novels. It was safe for her to assume people would think of it as fiction.

Today, nothing like that would happen. Kenali slipped into the limo with her daddy and sisters. She locked eyes with her daddy siphoning strength and discerning sadness. Momentarily, she saw something in his eyes resembling an abandoned little boy. She squeezed her eyes tightly together pleading with God to give them all strength to endure.

If I had been praying like this at the hospital, mama might still be alive.

The heat of the well of tears behind her lids was too much to contain. She turned her face to the window to release them. These tormenting thoughts were making losing her mother even worse than it already was.

As she opened her eyes, she began to scan the plethora of people already at the church. Although it warmed her heart to see how many people came to pay their last respects, she really didn't want to face any of them now.

Still shielded behind the tinted window of the limo, she let a few more tears sneak down her cheeks wiping them away swiftly. Then she took a deep inhale as she anticipated the driver swinging the door open.

"Remember to brace yourself," their dad warned again.

Simbol was already set to walk with their daddy, as she would be extra careful not to upset him even if that meant chewing on her tongue.

Divine was going to be escorted by her husband Gerald and two youngest boys while Kenali was going to walk with Divine's oldest son, Jamal. When she saw how his younger brothers sadly clung to him she opted to walk it alone. *Talk about reminder that I'm single.*

Once Kenali's feet hit the ground, she was shuffled through the crowd being passed from arm-to-arm of different people that thought their grief advice was more beneficial than the other. As overwhelming as it were, eventually she found her way to the front door of the church to join the family processional.

She stared at the back of her daddy's head daring him to look at her to give her some strength. When he did, his look shouted that he needed some too.

Once she turned the corner into the church to see her mother lying there amidst beautiful bouquets of flowers, she fully understood his look. Kenali's knees knocked. She hadn't prepared herself to see this version of her mother. She didn't look the same today as she had at the hospital minutes after her passing. Kenali had made excuses as to why she couldn't go view her mother's body beforehand. The real reason that only she knew was that guilt was ransacking her.

I wished I would've know that the lunch that I canceled would have been the last time I would have seen Mom alive.

Simbol cried out burying her face into the side of their daddy's arm. The sound was muffled. Kenali looked to the ceiling as her lips trembled uncontrollably.

"Oh, God, help," she whispered in desperation.

Kenali's focus was so deep on making it down the aisle without passing out that she never looked to see who had grabbed her arm in time to give strength. It was good he was buff. She needed to lean on them more than she thought. Attempting to keep her focus, she tightly squeezed his bicep burying her face into the side of his shoulder.

If I had married, this would be my husband instead of a cousin.

Kenali knew her mother would only remember the books, which she referred to as her babies. Success in the writing and speaking arena hadn't allowed for her to meet anyone special enough to bring home to the parents. Living in a small city in Alabama definitely didn't supply Kenali with a good picking. She felt as if she had accomplished nothing at all simply for the reason that her last name never changed and she didn't have a little person to look up to her to ask why his or her grandma doesn't come to visit anymore.

"Mama, I'm sorry," apologizing in the midst of heavy crying for being a social failure; for not praying; for not making the lunch date. She apologized for it all.

Now looking upon her mother, Kenali noticed what she thought was a smile on her face. That smile, which was probably imagined or there for another reason, interrupted her pity party giving her an escape from the guilt. She almost felt better.

"Thanks, Mama."

Kenali had to muster up the strength to come back to her mother's closed casket to do what she has always done best.

As she placed a kiss gently onto her fingertips to transfer to the casket, she smiled and began to read the poem that she had written specifically for this occasion.

"Gracious mother, we will release you but only into the Potter's Hands.

He will take you to a secret place without any more strict demands.

Even though we need you, God needs our best.

Into His hands, you go for a much-deserved rest.

His hands only will we trust

Such precious ashes-to-ashes and dust-to-dust."

Kenali had to break to sob. Then she felt a strong arm come around her waist for support. Once again, she did not look to see who it was. Their embrace was very familiar and it somehow gave her strength to carry on.

"Gracious mother, we will release you but only into the Potter's Hands.

On streets paved of gold is where you will eternally stand.

In those streets, one day we will count it all joy."

From the moment she fainted at the hospital to now, Kenali still hadn't figured out how they were supposed to count it all joy. She had even forgotten that she scribbled it into the poem before bitterly crying.

"But for us now, God has angels of comfort waiting to deploy.

We will always love and miss such a phenomenal woman as yourself.

But don't worry, for in our hearts we have for you just the perfect shelf."

Kenali paused mostly for the tears that had blurred her vision. She tussled in her mind how this was the most important poem she has ever done, yet while she was reading it, it felt elementary.

She thought back to when she was a little girl writing poems for her mom. Her mother would dress her up and set up a stage area in the living room for her to read her poems.

"You can finish this, Kenali," his familiar masculine voice gently whispered into her ear.

With one task at a time being all she could handle, she denied herself the need to quench her curiosity of why his voice was so familiar. Kenali wiped away the tears to finish.

"Gracious mother, we will release you but only into the Potter's Hands.

Into His hands many of our tears will land.

Tears of love mixed with the clay of many great words of you spoken,

Will create a glorious creation that will never again be broken."

That line was encouraging to Kenali to know sickness would never again touch her mom. The kidney failure had really taken a toll on her body although she never would admit it.

"God will break the mold when with you He is all done.

Only to present you as a special gift to His precious, sacrificing Son.

Gracious mother, you are released into the Potter's Hands."

As soon as she spoke the last word, some tension exited her body. Now she was released to see who had unselfishly been her personal motivator. As she looked up into such a handsome yet very familiar face, her knees waivered.

"Christian?"

She was so shocked to see him.

He definitely was not a cousin. Suddenly she was filled with more guilt and shame. How could he be here despite what she had done to him? If her mother could see him, Kenali was certain that she was in Heaven cheering for her favorite son-in-law that never was.

Exiting the church to go to the burial site, their dad praised them for how they handled the funeral.

"I know your mother is proud of you all for how you handled yourselves," he praised his daughters as the car drove along to the cemetery.

"Daddy, Mama would have loved that home going celebration. It was very upbeat which kept me from being as sad," Divine exclaimed.

"Yeah. It was. It helped me remember the good Christian life Mama lived," Kenali joined.

"Speaking of Christian, did you know he was coming Kenali?" Simbol smirked.

"No! I really didn't. He was right on time," Kenali smiled.

Simbol looked at Kenali with a devious look. If their dad wasn't in the car with them then she would pry all into Kenali's business about what really happened between the two of them.

Before they could continue the conversation, they arrived at the cemetery. Briefly, Kenali wondered how all the people beat them here. This was a smaller crowd than were at the church yet still a significant amount of people.

Kenali looked through the front window of the limo to see them removing the glowing white casket from the back of the hearse. Without warning, the rain began to pour from a perfectly sunny, blue sky that was speckled with white plush clouds.

As the pallbearers walked through the shower, Kenali got out looking up allowing the rain to shower down on her face.

Her family had already reached the tent. Other people began to scurry while some held their jackets or purses over their heads. Some even dashed to their cars to retrieve an umbrella; it was in vain. As soon as the pallbearers placed the casket upon its mount, the rain ceased.

Kenali's mind flashed back to when she was a little girl having a conversation about this same phenomena with her mama.

"Mama, it's raining outside but the sun is out. What does that mean?"

"It means that God is crying because something sad happened."

"Wow. God's tears can reach way down here."

"Yes, baby. God is everywhere. And you know what else?"

"What?"

"If you see a rainbow afterwards, that means God is making you a promise."

"What kind of promise?"

"God is promising you that you will not feel the sorrow that made Him cry."

Even though Kenali was only about 8 years old when they had that conversation, the remembrance was fresh. While she grew up to know there was some scientific explanation behind it, today Kenali believed that God was crying. He felt her pain although it still did not equal up to His.

As she looked towards the tent, she saw Simbol waving for her to come join them. She complied with her request.

This ceremony was brief which was best for her. Kenali just wanted to go home to deal with her emotions in private. As the family members placed a white rose upon her mother's casket, Kenali noticed that her daddy just stood there staring while holding his white rose tightly. She placed her hand softly on his back and said to him what she had to tell herself.

"Daddy, it's ok. She's with God now. You have to release her."

With that being said, he nodded his head in agreement while releasing his rose to fall with a dramatic slowness upon his wife's lowering casket.

As they turned to walk away, Kenali saw Christian had arrived. She wanted to go over to thank him but something wondrously amazing caught her attention to the point she had to stare. Kenali glared at the most perfect rainbow, with all of its radiantly colored glory, hanging in the sky as if it were a painting. She prayed that her mother was right about God making her a promise that she would never again feel this pain.

"Thank you for the promise, God. I really need it."

After the funeral, everyone gathered at the King's house. It was more like a family reunion than anything else with loads of relatives that had not seen each other in years.

Kenali noticed a couple of people that she remembered from high school across the room who luckily had not spotted her. She tried to stay in the background so she could sneak off to her room. Now was neither the time she really wanted to carry on casual conversation nor answer any more questions about how her mother passed. She had talked about kidney failure so much in the past few days she felt like a doctor herself.

While climbing the stairs, she looked across a sea of people to notice Divine and Simbol were cornered off separately with large clusters of people huddled around them. After carefully rescanning the room, she could not spot her father.

She reached the top of the stairs, starting down the hallway, hearing a bump inside her daddy's room; she knew that he had done exactly what she was attempting to do. She stood outside of his room silently investigating with her ear pressed against the door and her hand gently resting on the doorknob.

Attempting to see if she would hear the noise again landed her with a lump in her throat. She heard her father's voice downstairs answering someone who had called out to him.

Who is in Daddy's room?

Kenali rushed in with such a force, it startled the person who was inside of her parents' bedroom. The woman put her hand on her chest nervously breathing heavily.

"Oh dear, you scared me!" she exclaimed.

Kenali had this woman in a death stare.

"Really? I imagine I did. What are you doing in here anyway?"

Kenali interrogated the strange woman that was pilfering through her dad's room.

"I was just trying to help out by cleaning up a little bit," she shakily explained.

When Kenali looked down to see the woman clutching something tightly in her hand she responded accordingly.

"Yeah, I can see that you are. We just buried our mom and you want to rummage through our house like this. I'm calling the police."

"I'm sorry. It's really not what it seems like. I promise," the strange woman pleaded.

"Then you won't mind revealing what's in your hand," Kenali's tone was sharp and demanding.

"This is just my medicine. My name is on the bottle. See. I didn't steal anything," the woman begged for mercy.

Kenali was relentlessly trying to read the bottle the woman was holding up. It didn't belong to her parents but the name of the medication was familiar.

"That still doesn't explain why you're in my dad's room," Kenali's tone changed becoming more aggravated.

"Like I said, honey, I'm just trying to help out."

"We don't need any help in here. You need to excuse yourself from the house before I call the police."

Kenali stepped aside so that the woman could pass by her to leave. When she saw that she had reached the bottom of the stairs, she continued watching to make sure that she left the house. Reaching for the doorknob, the woman looked back up the stairs being met by Kenali's watchful eyes. Then she hurriedly left.

Kenali went back inside of her dad's bedroom to investigate if anything was out of order. It looked like everything was in its original place.

She looked on the dresser to see her mom's favorite pair of earrings. She traced the gold trimmed ruby teardrop earring with her finger. Trying not to cry, she moved on to observe the rest of the room. When she looked on the nightstand on her mom's side of the bed, tears rushed to Kenali's eyes. She saw her parents' black and white wedding picture. It had white creases across it due to wear and tear of time.

Kenali ran from the room slamming the door behind her. She burst into her room leaving the door open slinging herself across the bed as she did when she was a teenager having a hissy fit. Deeply sobbing, Kenali wondered when this pain would become manageable or if it ever would.

The most involved she had been with death was a few years ago, when Christian's mother died. Her heart went out to him for she never thought that his tears would find an end. This week she now fully understood the extent of his grief.

Divine peeked into Kenali's room watching her body shake from crying uncontrollably. She was screaming into the pillow her face was buried into. Divine struggled to fight back the urge to scream herself.

Walking fully into the bedroom, Divine gently closed the door behind her before crossing the room. Kenali was her baby sister and there was nothing that she could do to make the pain go away for either one of them. It wasn't like when they were young and Divine would put a Band-Aid on Kenali's scrapes and bruises. This pain was one the both were experiencing at the same time.

Rubbing Kenali's back was soothing to both parties.

"I know you're hurting, Kenali. This pain we're going to help each other through."

Divine continued to rub Kenali's back until she started to sit up. Kenali sat in the bed with her legs Indian style which made her look like a little girl all over again. She couldn't look at Divine but only stared at the pillow that still had the impression of her face. Kenali remained silent.

"I wanted to check on you. I heard the door slam."

Kenali looked up at Divine amazed that she closed the door with so much force.

"I was angry," Kenali pouted raising one eyebrow.

"Because Mom died?"

"No. Not then I wasn't. I'm not okay with her passing but there's nothing I can do about it now."

"You're right. It does hurt and we do have to accept it. I know God will bring peace to our hearts in due time."

"I certainly hope so." Then Kenali remembered the rainbow. "I know He will."

"So what were you so upset about that you rattled the walls downstairs?"

Kenali flinched at the thought of making that much noise. "I found this woman in Daddy's room talking about she wanted to help clean up," Kenali's anger was reemerging.

"Ms. Vera? I knew she looked spooked," Divine laughed.

Her laughter increased with the more she remembered the look on the woman's face as she fled from the house.

Kenali recognized the name from the pill bottle that she forced Ms. Vera to show her.

"What? You know her?" Kenali questioned.

"Yes. She went to dialysis with Mama. Sometimes Mama would bring her home with her and they would have lunch and drink coffee."

"Oh really? But why would she be in Daddy's room talking about she was trying to help clean up?"

"She probably was. She's old school. Back then, they helped out when someone was in need. Ms. Vera has a good heart. When I called the dialysis center to tell them that…"

Divine had to stop speaking because she did not want to say the rest of it. A lump filled her throat. She inhaled and exhaled deeply before continuing.

"When I told them that Mama had passed, they gave their condolences but they already knew. The nurse told me that when they told the other patients, that Ms. Vera took it the hardest and cried the entire time she was there."

"Oh, no. I was rough with her. I feel like such a jerk," Kenali replied shamefully covering her face. Her list of guilt was growing.

"You did right. No one is supposed to be in his room. I just understand in her case." Divine defended Kenali's actions

"It's like I got so angry thinking that someone was trying to take Mama's place and it's the day of the funeral. You know that heartless kind does exist."

Divine sucked her teeth.

"Girl, I know. It's two of them downstairs now."

Kenali flashed a sharp look at Divine.

"That look right there is why I told Simbol that I wasn't going to tell you. Keeping her cool is hard enough," Divine giggled.

"Are you serious? They're starting already?"

"Yes! Them she devils don't care about anybody's feelings. They're just out to get what they can get," Divine was disgusted.

"Let me change my clothes. I'll take care of them for coming in here with this foolishness," Kenali replied with complete seriousness.

"Kenali, you can't go down there and beat them old ladies up. You already scared poor Ms. Vera half to death," Divine halfheartedly joked.

"Watch me!"

They laughed at the thought. On the inside, Divine wanted to unleash Kenali and Simbol on the two that was being disrespectful. Mostly, Kenali was calm, peaceful and happy on the surface. But once irritated with someone, she has a chilling way of staring at that individual signifying that she doesn't play. Simbol's tactics were different and bolder.

The two sisters got over their laughing spell. Kenali opted out of changing her clothes deciding to change her shoes only. Deep down, she was glad that Divine came in to talk to her. It was what she needed.

The two went downstairs to interact with the visitors that were paying their last respects or disrespects. Of course, Kenali wanted those two pointed out. Divine did not have to say a word. Kenali spotted the she devils swarming around her dad like flies on a piece of raw meat. They pretended to be helpful by attempting to wait on him hand and foot. Kenali mentally gave her dad thumbs up because he was swatting them away as fast as they came.

"Did you see that?" Kenali asked.

Divine never allowed her stare to move away from what the women were doing.

"Did she put a chair right next to Daddy and sit in it?" Divine was looking appalled.

"Yep. I'm about to go handle—"

Kenali stopped mid-sentence and stride to watch Simbol in action. Divine and Kenali became overtaken in laughter as they watched Simbol ask the woman to get up so that she could sit next to her dad.

"Simbol's getting an all-expense paid shopping spree," Kenali happily proclaimed.

"I'll go halves with you," Divine giggled.

After an hour of talking, Kenali was once again ready for being alone. This time she was going to get her wishes.

Not being able to resist the urge to catch someone out of order, when she walked upstairs, she immediately rushed into her dad's room. It was empty this time. Gently closing the door, she went down the hallway into her room choosing to leave the door open so she could hear if anyone was sneaking around.

"I can't believe the nerve of those biddies," Kenali voiced her thoughts.

Then she shook her head in disbelief while walking into her bathroom.

Once again looking into the mirror seeing how much she looked like her mom, she could not resist the urge to touch her reflection. The tears came streaming down. As she cried, she walked around getting things situated for her midday shower. Hopefully the water would rinse away the results of the humidity as well as some of these tears.

Kenali chuckled wiping the tears from her eyes when the thought popped in her head of how she scared poor Ms. Vera.

"Note to self. Take her some flowers."

Thinking about what color flowers that Ms. Vera might like, she remembered the rainbow that she saw today. Kenali had always appreciated the rainbow as such a beautiful phenomenon that needed no explanation of its occurrence. It was beauty in the purest form. Moreover, it was even more beautiful today at the cemetery showing its comforting existence and purpose. The rainbow was a Holy symbol to show God's promise.

"I'm going to be ok."

Kenali encouraged herself by repeating it. Then she went back to the mirror and said it to her reflection. She was being her own motivational speaker.

Kenali realized the spoken word could be used either as a weapon or a tool; she used it as both. At least that is what she told her audiences. Speak to be a weapon of mass destruction to the things coming against you. Also, speak to be the tool to rebuild yourself after you have been torn down.

When she walked back into her room, she could hear through her opened bedroom door the volume of the multitude she happily left downstairs. She cringed from the thought of having to go back.

She grabbed her tablet and speakers sitting them onto the countertop of the bathroom. Quickly the thought to close her bedroom door came. She dismissed it.

Not knowing what musical mood she was in, she just chose all the music to play randomly. The types of music she listened to was a mixture ranging from classical to gospel and everything in between. She even had a couple of country songs in her playlist. If she liked it, she downloaded it.

The first song to come on was a song she had used recently at a workshop. "Better" by Jessica Reedy was proper and fitting for Kenali's mood.

Turning on the water in the shower, she anticipated how much better she was going to feel. The song's lyrics rang in her head as she held her hand underneath the running water. Life could be so bitter. Yes. That was true for her today.

Before peeling off her black Vera Wang two piece suit, she glanced herself over once more already agreeing this would be the last time she wore it. It was her favorite as it fit her curves professionally and powerfully while uplifting her mood enough to motivate anyone into greatness. She had worn it on a couple of corporate speaking engagements. The fabric was embroidered with rosettes which was balanced off with a black satin collar. She rubbed her hand up her sleeve slowly feeling the texture beneath her fingertips. *No*, she thought, *I'll never wear it again.* This suit in all of its splendor had become attached to her mom's death.

Then her thoughts became as random as her playlist.

I wonder if Christian will come over.

She shook her head to erase the thoughts about her ex-boyfriend. How she broke up with him made her feel guilty. Added to grief, she was not prepared for that type of torment. This was all so new to her until she did not know what to do, how to act, or how to feel.

Her final thought of Christian before letting him slide from her thinking was of how handsome he was at the funeral. In addition, she was grateful that he pushed their past to the side to be here for her now.

Inhaling deeply in an effort to suffocate those tormenting thoughts of the past, Kenali focused on the scent of the body wash. Its vanilla coconut aroma triggered another memory.

The family had vacationed in Jamaica a few years ago. Where they lodged, it was like the faint scent of fresh coconuts dancing enticingly on the breezes.

Christian was there too as he had already been accepted into the family. He and Kenali were inseparable. Her nephews had a new playmate since he was so athletic and active. The days were spent tossing the ball with the boys on the beach and sightseeing. The nights were just the two of them and steamy in nature.

Her body twinged from the memory of his touch. She buried her face in the shower's stream. Tears mixed with water that all went down the same drain. Kenali allowed herself to cry until she felt as if this session was done.

Pulling her face from the water, she felt an eeriness come over her. *Is someone in my room? I should have closed my bedroom door.*

Her heart started to beat harder than the hot memory of Christian caused it to. Kenali was seriously afraid.

Peeking out of the shower, she peered through the steam filled room. Immediately, she did not see anyone.

"My mind is playing tricks on me," she whispered.

Grabbing her towel, wrapping it around her body with quickness, she walked to go close her door to the bedroom. The closer she got she could hear some distinct individual's voices over all the other people downstairs. Seemingly, the voices had heightened as if more had joined into the already overbearing crowd.

Shutting out all the noise, she turned to go back to her bathroom to put on some comfortable clothing. As she turned into the bathroom, fear rushed over her once again. Pausing in her tracks, she knew this time there was a visual reason fear had manifested within her.

Remembering she had never left her balcony door open, she stood very still so she could think. Leaning back to peek around the bathroom doorframe, she caught a glimpse of an arm before the rest of the body moved completely out of view.

Who is that?

She ran to her closet to find refuge. Swapping the towel for some leggings and a t-shirt, she knew she would be able to maneuver better should it get physical.

One thing was for sure, she had enough of people inviting themselves into their personal bedrooms for one day. If it was another case like Ms. Vera, then she would apologize later. If it wasn't, she was about to let this person have it. They were about to receive all of her pent up anger she had from losing her mother to those vultures swarming around her dad.

She stepped out onto the balcony with the mindset to let this guy have it but did not get very far.

"Why are you—"

Those were the only words she was allowed to say. Walking with so much power, she could not stop when she saw who it was. She landed haphazardly into his arms. He embraced her in such a warm hug that her body almost went hopelessly limp. Fear became replaced by feelings of something missing now that Christian Jackson was actually here on her balcony.

"Hey, Kenali," Christian said in his deep masculine voice.

Kenali felt embarrassed once again as she looked at the sheepish smile on his face.

Before her stood a sight for sore eyes or a good pair of eyes for that matter. He had always been so extremely good looking that words would not properly describe him. His look was exotic and intoxicating. Most women of all races would just stare at him without saying a word. After one glimpse of his near perfection facial features atop a chiseled physique crowned with the perfectly shaped baldhead, women seem to lose all grace.

Even men recognized his good looks as he intimidated them whenever he walked into a room. Broad shoulders, perfect posture, well groomed, and 100 percent straight.

"Hey, Christian," she attempted to seamlessly transition. "I'm glad that you came by," her tone had calmed drastically.

"I could tell. It was something about the way that you were about to jump on me for being on your balcony."

Christian flashed his notorious one-sided smile exposing a set of straight toothpaste commercial white teeth. She missed him severely.

"Well, I had to figure out who was invading my privacy." It slipped. As soon as she heard the words that came from her mouth, she wished she could retract them.

"I'm sorry. I didn't mean to barge in but the door—"

Waving her hands and shaking her head, "No. I'm sorry. I didn't mean it like it sounded," Kenali apologized. "I really could use the company. Plus I was just thinking about you."

"You sure? I understand if you want to be alone, I can leave." Christian gestured towards the door.

He didn't catch her second slip of the tongue. If he had, the Christian she knew was certainly going to jive her every chance he could get about her thinking about him while she showered. He would know exactly what she thought of him if he knew that he was the lead male character in the erotic novels she used to write. But he wouldn't know that because she wrote underneath a pen name until her mother convinced her that if she had to change her name on the outside of the book because of what was on the inside of the book then why not change what's on the inside before it changed her.

Kenali gently pushed his arm down as if he was speaking nonsense. Christian was the same sincere man he was when they last saw each other. He was neither selfish nor conceited as his looks would warrant. He was a gentle giant.

"No. Don't go. Have a seat." Kenali pointed toward a seat next to the one that she began to lower herself into.

Christian looked before seating himself into the high backed patio chair. He crossed his leg placing his ankle on his knee. Instinctively his hand went to play with his shoestring of his black spit shined Stacy Adams.

Wow. He still does that.

"It's so crowded down there I don't blame you for hiding away," Christian commented. "So how are you holding up?"

Kenali paused before answering taking a moment or two to ask herself first.

"I think that it has to get better," she mimicked the song's lyrics. "If it doesn't, I don't know how I will function." Kenali sighed.

Sliding all the way back into the chair to allow it to embrace, she looked away from Christian not wanting him to see the tears swell in her eyes.

"Can I give you some advice?"

Kenali could not do any more than nod her head.

"Don't rush the process. Cry when you want to. Don't allow anyone to tell you how to grieve," Christian warned.

He was speaking from a place of familiarity. His words were riddled with regret.

Kenali smiled even though her eyes remained closed. She moved very little.

"Thank you. I needed that," Kenali paused.

Thinking about their past and how it was handled, she really did not want to say what was pressing her although it was forcing its way out. It had been a long time coming for her to say this.

"I'm sorry that I wasn't a better girlfriend to you when you needed me the most. And now you're here helping me and—"

A tear seeped from the corners of her eyes.

"Look at me, Kenali."

When she never did, Christian dropped his leg sitting up straight. He reached over to touch her hand but she still didn't respond to him. He slid from his chair, kneeling before Kenali resting his hands gently on her knees. When they made eye contact, he continued.

"Don't add to your grief by digging up old stuff."

"But I didn't understand how to console you when your mom died," Kenali cried.

"How could you know?"

"But I could have done more."

"You did what was important. You allowed me to talk about it. I've never held anything in my heart against you concerning that." Christian squeezed her knees to reassure her.

Kenali sniffled. Christian's heart ached for her. He knew exactly how she was feeling.

"Thank you for your help."

"I'm glad that I can be here for you. If there's anything that I can do to help you after today, let me know. I mean it, Kenali. Anything."

"Thanks for the offer. I may have to call you up on it."

"Don't hesitate to do so. Matter of fact, here's my card. Call me anytime. Day or night." Christian was sincere in what he said to her.

"Thanks," spoken very timidly while staring at the card.

Kenali looked at the New York address. It confirmed what she had heard about him abruptly leaving Alabama when they broke up. She didn't just drive him across state lines but she attempted to drive him from her heart's memory. It was impossible.

Why did we break up?

Kenali scrambled to control her thoughts.

"So how long are you going to be in town?' Kenali questioned.

"A little over a week. It's been awhile since I've been home to Bama. So I'll check the place out to see how much it has changed while I'm here," he smiled at the thought.

"Welcome home. If you need a tour guide to show you all the changes, my services are available," Kenali joked forcing a smile wiping the tears from her eyes with the sleeves of her shirt.

"I will definitely take you up on that. It's been a minute," Christian returned the smile sensing her change of mood.

The two went on for hours catching up on old times. A lot had happened in their personal lives in the three years since they parted. Kenali's suppressed feelings towards Christian returned full bloom the moment she laid eyes on him. However in their conversation that night, his words were sure and she knew he had moved on. She couldn't blame him.

She was thankful for him being there for her now. In the middle of the night she awoke to find herself neatly tucked into her bed. The more she became aware she began to remember that she dosed off on the balcony. She only awakened slightly when Christian gathered her body into his arms. She didn't resist him but laid her head on his shoulder as he carried her. The coolness of the night was far too intoxicating for her grief weary body to fight. It was as if this sleep was drug induced.

Now as her half closed eyes scanned the room from her bed, she saw Christian stretched out on the chaise lounge across the room. With a gentle smile, she peacefully dozed back off into a sleep that will be the best she's had since her mom's passing. Christian's presence made her feel safe.

Christian drove back to his hotel room thinking about how haunting Kenali's cries were when she slept. As a man there was nothing he could do; this time he couldn't be the solution to Kenali's problem.

As he drove, he looked around at all the changes that had taken place in the city he once called home. It looked like so different. He had sworn that he would never set foot in this place again. He already knew better than to say never.

Just as the city had grown, so had Kenali. She was a very different person not just age wise. Since their talk, there was something about her that made him want her back even more. Christian had never stopped loving her regardless of how his heart cracked when she pushed him away. He wanted so greatly to question her yesterday but he knew better. Besides, he was here to be of support to her not to bring up old pain.

Going to the funeral brought back memories of his own mother's funeral. That was a hard place for him especially being an only child without a father. Today, after the graveside service, he lingered around placing fresh flowers on his mom's grave, sitting there having a little chat letting her know he was back for a visit.

When he walked out the cemetery, he passed the fresh mound that belonged to Mrs. King. He could not believe she was gone. She was his cheerleader as well as another mom to him the entire time he and Kenali dated. Christian knew Mrs. King was always in his corner when he and Kenali was having a little lover's spat. Mrs. King encouraged him by patting his arm and placing a nice sized piece of homemade pie or cake in front of him. That made everything alright for him; Kenali would just have to take time to calm down. It was something about knowing that her mom was giving him special treatment that made her flare up a little more.

"I don't think Kenali likes when you pay me attention like this."

Christian made the statement more towards Kenali than to Mrs. King in hopes to provoke her to jealousy. Kenali rolled her eyes looking away. Christian smirked.

"She'll be alright. She acts like that because she's my baby girl," Mrs. King replied while rubbing the back of Kenali's head.

Kenali made a half attempt to swat at her mother's hand.

"I don't know about that. She's going to take it out on me later just like she always does," Christian continued as if Kenali was not in the room.

"Let me take care of her. I know just how to coax her. Even from the time she was a beautiful baby, I knew just what to do when she got, you know—fussy. I'm such a proud mom and so grateful that God blessed me with such wonderful children." Mrs. King winked an eye at Christian behind Kenali's back.

"You do know that I'm right here in the same room with you two," Kenali spoke in defense of herself. "And I'm not being, you know—fussy. I'm just being quiet. It's true what they say. You can learn a lot about people when you're quiet. I'm learning things about you two right now." Kenali shook her head in a shame on you manner.

Mrs. King and Christian looked at one another erupting into laughter. They both knew that Kenali's speaking was her way of alerting them she had softened to the point of no longer holding onto what previously had her panties in a bunch.

Mrs. King always did know how to referee the two of them. He guessed she had no control over Kenali when she dropped the mega bomb on him three years ago.

Now walking into the room, heading straight for the closet, Christian thumbed through his limited selection of clothing he had brought. He was thankful he remembered how humid Alabama could be while he was packing.

He selected a red shirt that was slightly fancier than a tee yet just as comfortable. Holding it up to inspect if it needed ironing, he decided against the extra work and paired it with some khaki cargos. Briefly, he thought of how Kenali would tell him that red was a color that looked wonderful against his smooth brown complexion. A sly smile came upon his face.

Becoming more serious, he kicked off his Stacy Adams so that he could strip out of the black suit which was somewhat clinging to him already. It was only 10a.m. and he had only been without A/C walking across the parking lot.

"Whew. It feels good to be out of this." He had worn it almost twenty-four hours since he didn't foresee spending the night at Mr. King's house.

Christian stood in front of the air conditioner allowing it to blow cool breezes across his shirtless, clammy body. This moment felt so good that he stood with his head back and hands resting on his hips. He wanted the airflow to reach his armpits and everywhere.

While standing there, enjoying the moment, he thought of the conversation he'd had in the wee hours of the morning with Mr. King after he caught him slipping out his daughter's bedroom. He could imagine how it looked with his dress shirt unbuttoned and hanging out. He was careful to explain that he didn't do anything to disrespect his house. However, Mr. King waved him off because he knew his character.

It had been awhile since they had talked man-to-man. Christian always gleaned so much from Mr. King since he viewed him as more of a father than his own. After he had cooled down enough, he returned his head to a more natural position just in time to see the last few strides of a woman crossing the parking lot coming into the hotel. He placed his face into the sheer white curtain until his head met the window. He thought of how that small glimpse of this woman looked familiar to him.

"No. It couldn't be her."

Dismissing the thought from the impossibility of being that particular person, he finished undressing opting to take a shower to undo what the heat had done plus work out some of the kinks in his neck caused by sleeping on the much too little chaise lounge.

Christian placed his hand under the running water to gauge the temperature. He wanted the water to be slightly cool but with enough warmness to not give him the chills. When it was just right, he pulled the knob up to transfer the water to the showerhead.

Stepping underneath the stream of refreshing water, he allowed his thoughts to be of what he was going to do the rest of the day as well as the rest of the time he was going to be in Alabama. Outside of being with Kenali, he knew that he wanted to go visit his cousin Lane. After all, Lane is the reason he knew Mrs. King had passed.

❧ | ❧

He thought on the day in which he was sitting in his office when the phone call came to his cell. Seeing Lane's name flash up on his screen allowed him to answer it the way two cousins that grew up together would.

"What up cuz?" Christian yelled into the phone not sounding like the Advertising professional he was.

"Well, man, you know I'm good. But I needed to holler at you about something important."

"You need advice on how to handle the woman that's chasing after you?" Christian joked.

"Naw man. It's something more serious than that."

Christian poised himself based on Lane's voice. He sensed this was not going to be the regular man trash talking conversation they had from time to time. Almost afraid to ask, his mind searched of possible things of what it could be about before he allowed the question to part his lips.

"What's wrong?" Christian stiffened.

"Are you in your office alone?"

"Yes." Christian's mouth dried. He put his elbow on his desk and placed one side of his face in the palm of his hand. *This couldn't be good news at all*, he thought.

"Your beloved Mrs. King passed away," Lane pushed out.

Christian's heart failed him. Pain jolted into his memories as they all flashed before him. It was moments later before he was able to speak.

"Christian, are you still there?"

Christian paused before answering. His heart ached greatly. Tears were forming in his eyes. Christian wanted nothing more than to crawl underneath his desk to shield his pain from being seen through the glass walls of his office. He didn't know how to deal with it publicly. The only thing he could think of was to ask a question.

"Kenali died?"

"No! Not her. Her mama died," Lane reassured.

Christian straightened himself. Hope had returned to him then anger.

"Man, stop calling me from that raggedy cell phone," Christian yelled.

"Whatcha talking about?"

"Your phone was breaking up. All I heard was your love King passed away."

"Oh. My bad. You was about to cry too wasn't you? Tell the truth, shame the devil," Lane joked.

Sniffing to gain his male composure, "About to cry? I was almost under the desk. But I can't believe Mrs. King is gone."

"She was a great woman. You are coming to the funeral right? I'll get you all the details."

"You think I should come?" Christian did not know if it would be appropriate for him to come since the relationship between him and Kenali had been broken.

"Man, you better get on the first thing smoking heading this way. It's not about you and Kenali. It's about paying your last respects to a phenomenal woman who accepted you like her own son and nurtured you when auntie died," Lane passionately voiced his opinion.

"Ok. I'm booking my flight now."

Adrenaline now flowed through his body causing him to feel the instinctive need to rush to Kenali's side to extend a comforting shoulder to lean on even though he was not sure how she would receive him. He questioned it while he made the travel arrangements, when he packed his bag and even when he reached the rental car desk at the airport after he landed in sweet home Alabama. He decided to ask the clerk at the counter to get a woman's perspective on the matter.

"Excuse me but could I ask you a question?"

The look on the clerks face lit up even more when Christian spoke to her. "Certainly, sir," she expressed with a new glee.

"I need a woman's point-of-view on something. I know that you're busy so I'll briefly give you the scenario."

"I'll assist you if I can," the woman responded back.

"Ok, here goes."

Christian hurriedly gave his entire story to a strange woman and eagerly waited on her answer. However, the response he got was not the one he was expecting. The clerk had burst into tears while Christian stood there wide-eyed and bewildered about what he had done.

"Are you ok? I didn't mean to make you cry," he hesitantly spoke.

"It's not you," she responded full of tears hiding her face in the palms of her hands. "When my mother died, my own fiancé didn't make a two hour drive to come to her funeral and you came so far to a woman that dumped you three years ago."

The clerks sobbing heightened and Christian, despite feeling slightly offended by the statement of being dumped, felt like this was a good time to interject.

"Well, you see sometimes people are for us or they are not right for us." *You are with a jerk*, is what he really wanted to say.

He paused because he noticed that with everything he said, her sobbing got worse. He then looked back to see the disgruntled looks that the people in the line behind him had on their faces.

"I'm so sorry that I'm making things worse for you. I think that it's best that I stop talking and just leave."

"It's not you. We're getting married in a couple of weeks and I just keep feeling like he's not the one."

Being a man, Christian knew this marriage was going to be a big mistake.

Sighing heavily, "If you're feeling it, then he's not. I'm no counselor but I am a man. If he doesn't support you in your pain then he'll not be there period. I'm the last one to break up a relationship but don't stay in one that you're not happy with. Know your worth and wait on one that's going to value you."

"Okay," she muttered.

While she was wiping her face with a Kleenex, Christian blinked twice and scanned her face over to see if she was going to be alright. He felt a relief when she smiled and said, "Thank you."

He dared not ask but assumed the answer to his question was two thumbs up. He knew exactly what he was supposed to do when he sat inside of the rental car and turned the ignition.

Now in the shower, his thoughts were interrupted as he allowed his listening to become keener. He thought that he heard a knock on his door. Peeking his head out the shower to listen, he found he was right. He thought on who it could be as he turned the water off reaching for a towel to wrap around himself. By the time he looked out the peephole, he saw no one. He opened the door sticking his head out looking both ways not seeing a soul in sight. He just wrote it off that someone might have been knocking on the door next to his room.

Going back into the bathroom, looking into the mirror his eyes fell onto the tattoo that he had transformed into something less painful. It once was the name Kenali etched into the left side of his chest resting over his heart. When they would workout together, he would pull his shirt off making his chest jump and then make some corny statement that would make her giggle every time. But about a year ago he decided to stop tormenting himself and had it transformed into a cross. And the truth being told, it wasn't any less painful because as long as he had a memory he would always know what its beginning was.

Covering it did however help in the dating world or anywhere he would have to take off his shirt. Even at the gym, he no longer had to explain who Kenali was and how to pronounce it. Nobody asked about the cross he guessed out of fear that he was going to preach to them. They did not have to worry about that since he was not in the church himself.

As a matter of fact, he hadn't been to church in years with the last time being when he was living here. No. He couldn't preach to anybody especially since he kept trying to have sex with Kenali the way they would before she gave her life to the Lord. If he knew then like he knew now, he would have stepped back allowing her to blossom into the woman she was becoming.

Especially with the alternative being horrible. The dating scene was not like when he and Kenali first met. These women today seemed desperate which was a nightmare knowing that out of desperation they would do anything to get and keep a man. Kenali on the other hand did not even give him her number when they met. When he first saw her, she was like inhaling a breath of fresh air.

Kenali was a walking billboard of perfection. Christian did not know if it was that she was perfect in every eye or just perfect in his. Everything about her made his heart go on a speeded race.

She was gorgeously draped in beautiful brown skin that had a reddish undertone that smoothly covered her 5'7 frame with a sheer decadence managing to slope her every curve. She walked down the sidewalk with confidence not cockiness which was even more attractive to him.

That was the first time he figured out what it meant to be left speechless. Although unable to speak, he knew that he would have to catch up with her and hope that his mouth would not fail him at what he knew to be the most important moment of his life thus far.

By the time he finished talking to her, he decided to ask her for her number so he could call her. She graciously gave him something so unexpected.

"I don't give my number out to strangers. If perhaps we were to meet again, then maybe."

And with that she gave him a precious smile that melted his heart from that day forward as she walked away. Rejection never sounded so good to him until she did it. She was going to play hard to get and he was definitely up to the chase.

His desire to know more about her led him to play detective. She had come out of Spoken Café therefore he went in to ask a few questions. Finding out that she was a regular, he planned his next visit and seating arrangement.

The next time Kenali was predicted to visit, Christian was already seated inside at the table that she always sat at. He returned the smile that she sent to him as she sat down in front of him and began the first conversation of many.

Today, as he drove back to the King's home, he passed by Spoken Café smiling at the thought of their meeting. He even passed by several of their constant hangouts. Looking down one of the streets, he could see the silhouette of the park in which he and Kenali went to many jazz concerts around this time of year. With the combination of the jazz bellowing and nature in full bloom, their love was alive.

Their love was beyond so much that it crossed over into passion. He often desired to look into her face when she allowed herself to lye back on the grass with her eyes closed being blanketed by the emotions the music persuaded her to have.

He loved to trace her facial features with his eyes starting with the corner of her pecan shaped eyes. His next stop would be to slope down her nose letting his eyes befall upon such a magnificent pair of full lips that double arched to orchestrate their thickness. Not only were the lips beautifully thick but so was she. She was delightfully curvaceous. By the end of the night, he would trace those curves with his eyes and hands until passion would explode all over again.

However, that was then before he learned the painful lesson of when people are changing, respect their wishes. His inability to do so is why he primarily and painfully concluded that he could not fault her. That's why he still loved her in secret from a distance. Although there were still those times in which he wanted to know the real reason.

He pulled into the driveway admiring the beautiful 2-story brick home that the King's owned. He had been through those doors so much it felt as if he was walking into his own home.

When he turned to close the car door, he saw a car slowly passing by. The female driver looked a lot like the woman he saw at the hotel but the tinted windows and glare from the sun prevented him from getting a good look.

"Is that Julia?" Christian asked himself.

Reason told him to dismiss the thought. Julia was in New York and it would be senseless for her to be here.

"Hey you," Kenali's voice came from the corner of the house.

Christian looked around to see Kenali standing to the right of the house looking beautiful as ever in a yellow sundress. It innocently flaunted her curves and allowed enough sun to peer through to reveal a shadow of her silhouette. *This is going to be hard*, he thought.

"Hey back at you," his smile was boyish.

"Thank you for staying the night. I slept really well because you were here," Kenali shyly lowered her head smiling as she playfully slid her sandal across the top of the blades of grass.

"Anything you need, Kenali. Remember that."

Christian returned a smile. After the time they had been apart, right now felt like the very first time he met her. He missed her more than he thought. Hushing his arising feelings to focus on his true purpose of being here, he told himself that helping Kenali to cope with her mother's death would have to take precedence over his deep longing for her.

Scanning the crowd for his daughters, finding all but Kenali, Mr. King knew he had to get away from this crowd for a moment. Divine and Simbol seemed to be handling their conversations well. He now needed to go somewhere to get himself together. He was willing to bet Kenali was upstairs in her old room doing the same thing.

Mr. King just couldn't stomach anymore of this circus. This was the second day the house was full of guests. He couldn't believe it. Normally, just the day of the funeral and then after that people gave the family space to grieve.

He had to watch Simbol play musical chairs with this foolish old lady who kept groping his arm. If she touched him one more time, he felt like he was going to give her a real good southern cussing out. Divine gracefully got another woman told about making advances toward him already. He could only fathom what Kenali has said or done to these hoard of women that was after the spot of being the new Mrs. King.

He appreciated how his girls were protecting him but in his mind, even though he knew it would be like this, they should not have to do it.

"These old women need to sit down somewhere," he spoke aloud primarily to himself. The height of all the

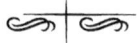

voices wouldn't allow anyone else to hear him without being in his immediate presence.

He climbed the stairs to go to his room. Placing his hand on the doorknob, he hesitated. He rubbed his hands through his sideburns regretting that his wife would not be on the other side of the door when he opened it. Mr. King walked into the room knowing one day that this was going to get easier. Just not today.

He walked across the room to go into his bathroom when he spotted through the window his daughter that was missing in action. Kenali was walking outside in the backyard with Christian.

"Honey, do you see that? Your baby girl's out there with Christian just like you always wanted," Mr. King paused to fight back tears. "I just didn't know this was going to be what it took to make it happen."

He grabbed the wall for balance before continuing into the bathroom. After returning, he came to his wife's side of the bed seeing a picture of them on their wedding day. The girls had it restored a couple of years ago. He picked it up, tracing every detail in his sweet Pastoria's face. Tears began to flow uncontrollably from his eyes to land on the frame.

"I miss you, ol' girl. Always thought I was going to be first to go. But I guess that wouldn't be fair either for you to have to feel this pain."

Mr. King grabbed onto the thick round bedpost and lowered himself onto the bed still with the picture frame in his hand. He couldn't break his stare from the woman who he never broke his vow; to love in sickness and in health until death does its part.

"So, Kenali," Christian reluctantly began, "how did your mom pass?"

Kenali gathered her thoughts. Then she blurted out the same preprogrammed answer everyone else received.

"Complications due to kidney failure."

Realizing Christian wasn't everyone else, she gave more detail. "Well as you know, a few years ago, she was diagnosed with kidney failure and had been having dialysis three times per week until a kidney could be donated."

"She never got a call about a donor being found?" Christian curiously questioned.

"Yes. The call came in about 2a.m. But she told us that she turned it down because she was afraid of the surgery. I really wished she would have had accepted the kidney."

Kenali looked off into the distance. Christian replayed a memory in his mind to be able to console Kenali.

"Not having the surgery could have actually extended her life."

"I'm sorry. I forgot your mom passed during heart transplant surgery. We don't have to talk about this now."

"No, Kenali. This is actually helpful to you. I have come to a point of being ok with what happened to mom. It's not a fresh pain like yours. I'm here to help you."

Kenali thought about Christian's statement for a moment syphoning hope from it. She knew that one day her tears would not be as constant as they are right now. Plus, there were some things surrounding her mom's death that nobody else knew that she wanted to get out of her system. They were eating away at her on the inside.

"Christian, I need to tell you something that I can't tell my family. They would probably get mad with me."

He stiffened anticipating what could be so bad. "Ok. You can tell me."

Kenali sat down on a stump next to the tree in which they were standing beneath. She struggled with saying what was on her mind. Actually, it consumed most of her thoughts in a way that was about to drive her crazy. She had to tell someone. Besides, they were well out of earshot of anyone at the house.

She tugged at the grass uprooting some of it. She licked her lips, sighed and began to talk.

"The day Mama died I had come by the house earlier that morning but I was supposed to come back for lunch," Kenali stopped. She covered her mouth and closed her eyes.

Christian rubbed her shoulders knowing what she had to say was painfully robbing her of a proper grieving period. It riddled grief with guilt. Kenali gathered herself enough to start talking again.

"She called and said lunch was almost ready. Then I told her that I couldn't make it because I was working on something. But I would come by after she got out of dialysis that afternoon," Kenali sobbed. "The only thing is, that afternoon I didn't get a call from her. I got one from the dialysis center saying that she had been rushed to the hospital."

Kenali wiped her eyes with the tail of her sundress leaving wet splotches that turned the fabric in those areas a deeper yellow.

"I missed the last lunch with my mom because I was writing. What kind of a daughter am I?"

Kenali recognized that she didn't feel any better by letting it out. She only felt that Christian was going to judge her for dismissing her mom to write a poem. And just like that poem burned in her brain that day, the guilt burned mightier each and every day since then.

Christian kneeled down on the ground in front of Kenali looking up into her face. He rubbed both of her shoulders causing her limp body to sway in whichever direction his hands proposed. The right thing to say swirled around his brain until it came to him.

"You are the daughter she created you to be. Your mom knew you were a writer and she loved that about you. Remember how she would encourage you to write and how her eyes would sparkle when she saw you perform or speak. She's not holding anything against you for missing lunch. She would never want you to grieve over that or even over her for too long."

After his words began to sink in, Kenali did start to feel slightly better. Christian was right. Her mother was happiest when Kenali was doing what she did best. It pleased her when any of her daughters were operating in their gifting. Divine is in design, Simbol is catering and Kenali is the writer.

Kenali reached forward to hug Christian. If her mother saw this moment, she would be grinning from ear-to-ear as she always did root for him.

Although it felt good to hug Christian, a small battle began to erupt inside of her. It had been so long since she was able to hold him other than inside her mind that now she wasn't handling it well. Regret as well as other emotions was coming forth.

Before any of it could seep in, Kenali sprung to her feet almost throwing Christian backwards.

"What's wrong? What do you see?" Christian inquired.

Kenali's look didn't match that of someone that was afraid but as if she was about to conquer something.

"I feel like running," she exclaimed.

"Running?"

"Yes. I feel like running fast as I can through this field just like I did when I was a child without a care in the world."

Christian understood. "Then run."

"The last one to make it to the tree on that hill right there is a rotten egg." Kenali left being the thirty-one year old responsible woman to regress back to childhood.

Then she almost took off like lightning but he grabbed her by the wrist. She looked at Christian to see what the problem was.

"I'm going to beat you there," he said.

Christian sprinted off ahead of her and she chased him giggling as if they were two little children at playtime. While she ran behind him as fast as her sandals would allow, he turned around to taunt her by running backwards.

Kenali needed this moment to run away from everything that bothered her. She ran free of the death of her mom, the regrets of missing lunch, and even the regrets of letting Christian go. Only if she could run forever then she would never have to face any of it. Having to deal with all of it at one time was more than she could bear. Therefore, for now she ran away.

Christian walked into his hotel room and began to descend face down towards the bed. When he woke up the next morning, he accepted he was a lot more exhausted than he had previously perceived. Kenali almost ran him to death.

Realizing that he had fallen asleep fully clothed, he got undressed, put on some shorts and headed out for his morning jog. The sun was just starting to wake up to fulfill its purpose of lighting the earth. He decided to head to the park in which he always favored running through. It gave him the sense that he was on a rugged trail although it was a paved walkway overshadowed by trees. He liked being surrounded by nature inhaling and exhaling the freshness that it produced. It was great being home. This was an opportunity to breathe again.

After his jog, upon arriving back at the hotel, he went to the lobby to get some apple juice to quench his thirst before returning to his room. While strolling through the lobby, he looked to his left to catch another glimpse of the woman that kept popping up yesterday looking like Julia. Today he was almost certain that it was not her.

The hairstyle and color was much different from how Julia wore her hair. Her extremely straight bangs sat upon her dark high fashion shades that covered a large portion of her face. The rest of her blonde hair was past shoulder length cascading to cover up some of the side of her face causing a mysteriousness to be about her. Even though he couldn't see her entire face, there was something cold and dark about this woman. Julia's only problem was being excessively clingy.

After getting onto the elevator, he wished he had caught up with her to get a closer look. The need to know led him to press the button to return to the lobby.

His brief ride made him feel like a kid playing in the elevator. Now as it opened up into the lobby, he immediately began his search of the mysterious woman. He couldn't find her anywhere.

"Excuse me. Do you know where the woman that was sitting over there went to?" He asked the attendant who was cleaning the breakfast area.

She smiled and shook her head, "No," before continuing her task.

He searched on his own to no avail. Then he abandoned his mission since he felt foolish for doing so.

There was no reason for her to be here, he thought while swiping his room key. Christian once again dispelled the nonsense from his mind replacing it with thoughts of how good a long hot shower was going to be.

Now in the shower, he continued planning his day that he mentally started while jogging.

Feeling refreshed, Christian drove through the city without missing a beat. He knew exactly where to turn. Even the new developments were not able to trip him up. He had traveled this route many times before. He had not been gone long enough to forget certain things.

When he drove past Kenali's house, it looked familiar to him yet like a strange place due to a large amount of landscaping. He had to admit the layout accented her home very well. Laughing aloud, he remembered how terrified she was of small animals such as frogs and lizards. So many times, he had to come over to rescue her from one being on her door preventing her from leaving. That was until she saved up to have a garage built onto her home. The thought alone caused negative questions to begin to surface into his head. What if Kenali had only softened towards him because she was grieving? Christian winced at the idea that once Kenali got to a place that she could manage her pain she would give him the boot again. Or, even worse, what if she had someone who was a jerk that chose not to show up like the fiancé of the woman at the rental car company? Kenali, as far as Christian remembered about her, wasn't the one to become tangled up with those types of men.

Calming down, he reminded himself of how he came to pay his last respects not to rekindle their love.

Besides, he had dated other women since they went their separate ways and thinking Kenali should be alone was a bit territorial.

However, those thoughts kept relentlessly bombarding him. His heart began to beat faster. It wasn't anxiety; it was anger. He pressed his foot harder onto the accelerator needing to get to his destination quicker.

No longer trying to calm himself, Christian began examining his feelings. He felt stupid for still loving Kenali. After all, he thought, if she could push him away so easily then maybe she had one of those church guys already wooing her. He could have been absent from the funeral because he was out of the country doing some mission work. Now Christian was enraged.

His mind began to scan over the relationships that he had been in since they were together last. Most of them he had sabotaged because he was trying to make them measure up to Kenali. Julia was one of them. Yes. She was clingy and slightly weird but he could have made it work if Kenali wasn't always hopefully in the back of his head.

He pounded the steering wheel. Then again. He repeated this action until he felt better. Before becoming engulfed, he saw that he was approaching his first destination.

As he pulled over, his feelings of anger were receding if only a little. While looking at the entrance, he slightly felt guilty for being angry but he knew he would find the peace of mind he needed within the walls of nature.

Christian hoped the area was the same. Walking the trail, he indulged in the memory of the first time that he and Kenali stumbled upon the perfect area that was deemed as their oasis from that day forward.

It was then when they walked the narrow pathway hand-in-hand as he led them to the opening which was a joyful shock to their eyes. It was as if they had been wandering in the desert looking for water stumbling upon a real oasis. The sight was so unrealistically beautiful that they had to blink twice. It was hard to believe something so spectacular was hidden deep in the forest with only a tiny trail as evidence of its existence.

Today he walked the trail alone consumed by enough anger to wonder if the spot, which once belonged to them, was at any other time reassigned to Kenali and another. He forcefully swatted the leaves that hung in his pathway.

Then he came to the opening. It was as breathtaking as it was when they first discovered it. His optic sensors were greeted by the same beautiful pond that sparkled beneath the sun's rays as if it were filled with diamonds. The pond was surrounded by lush green grass that seemed to have been manicured and painted a storybook green. The other vegetation looked strategically placed in its spots by someone with an eye for design. As he looked in amazement, his anger turned to flee. This place was Heaven on Earth.

There was a mother and baby deer standing by the water taking a drink. The mother looked up at him as he walked towards the water. She darted away with baby hot on her trail.

Christian's mind was in constant flashback. Back then, he and Kenali were so amazed at the sight of this place that just like little children they took off running toward the water. They began dancing in circles while holding hands and falling on the ground from dizziness. They felt like kids again who were allowed to freely enjoy themselves. This spot had to have been designed for the sole purpose of making people forget about the troubles of life.

Instantaneously it made Christian and Kenali forget that this area must belong to someone. They didn't even care if they were trespassing. This was a biblical moment as they were allowed to have a glimpse of what Adam and Eve felt inside the Garden of Eden—before they got kicked out.

Today, it took a lot for him to keep himself under control. He inwardly beat himself up for still caring for a woman that had obviously moved on. Justifying his actions, he was never given the opportunity to know why they were over. Now he felt feminine for needing closure. He laughed at himself.

Reaching the water's edge, he started to have a conversation with the reflection of the man he saw looking back at him.

"You're a handsome man. Why are you so caught up on this one woman? You should have a really good woman on your arm and not be wishing for a ghost."

As he stood there scolding himself something rose up on the inside of him in defense of his actions. Briefly, he almost thought that he had lost his mind. Christian had heard before that people are crazy when they talk to themselves and even crazier when they answer themselves. He felt like he was going to be on a new list since he felt an argument coming up.

"But I still love her. It's my fault that we're not together. I guess."

"Sometimes talking into the water does help."

At the sound of another voice coming from behind him, Christian almost jumped into the water. He thought he was all alone. Then sheer embarrassment replaced fear. However, when he looked around into the blue-gray, age dimmed eyes of the one that was speaking to him; he knew his actions were understood.

"Women can drive you crazy like that. I talked to myself all the time before I married this great gal."

Christian looked at the aged couple who seemingly shared timeless love. Their arms intertwined as they stood side-by-side. The man had on a pair of baggy overalls with a red bandana hanging out of his left pocket. It matched his short-sleeved plaid shirt and red cap, which had seen a few tours of duty. It sat atop his head with his stringy gray hair that was longer on one side. Christian was willing to bet that when he didn't have the hat on that he combed it over to cover a bald spot.

His wife matched his attire with her denim capris, red button up shirt, and a khaki floppy straw hat. Underneath its brim, he could see that her eyes were smiling towards him.

Christian warmed on the inside and it spilled over onto his face while he nodded his head in greeting to the couple.

"It's that obvious that I'm having woman troubles?"

"Yep. Pretty much."

The man was now close enough to extend his hand to shake Christian's. The two men shared a firm handshake.

"Wow. I was really trying to keep it under control."

"Sometimes you just have to get it out in order to keep it under control. If you let it build up, then you're a ticking time bomb waiting to happen."

Christian could testify to that as he remembered his roller coaster ride of anger earlier.

"So how long and how often did you dump all of your cares into the water?"

"Until I made up my mind that I was going to plant my feet and fight for her."

"Fight for her?" Christian asked.

He wondered how that could be applied to his situation when he didn't know all the facts about Kenali's relationship status.

"Well I'll leave you two alone so that you can talk man-to-man."

She excused herself walking around to the other side of the pond to begin setting up for a picnic.

"That's my best and only gal for 50 years."

"50 years? That's a long time. How did you survive?"

Christian thought about that length of time with one person. How was that possible? How could he have that?

"It's not always been easy but we were there for each other regardless of what happened."

Christian envied that. *Regardless of what happened* rung in his head repeatedly.

"So is that the recipe to staying married for so long?"

"Yep. Plus love," the man simply replied.

Christian tried to wait for his elderly advisor to say something else but he never did.

"And that's all?"

"Yep."

This time the answer was shorter. Christian became slightly irritated. How was he supposed to learn something from these short answers?

"Please explain it to me. I really need to know."

"First off, are you already married or are you thinking about asking her?"

Christian pondered on how to explain their relationship status.

"Well, right now, neither. We broke up a couple of years ago."

"Couple of years ago?"

"Yes. Three to be exact."

He must think I'm crazy or a stalker, Christian thought.

"Can't get her out of your mind?"

"No."

"Well, she must be mighty special."

Is she? She got me speeding out here beating up my car and tearing down trees.

"Yes, she is," Christian replied.

"Then plant your feet and fight for her."

"I don't quite understand what you mean by planting your feet."

"Stand on your principle. In your case, that's your love for her. Don't ever let it go and let her know it. You have to stand your ground and show her how special she is to you. Women want to be cherished, desired, and made a fuss over. They think that if you won't fight for them, that they don't mean nothing to you."

"But she broke up with me," Christian defended.

"Apparently she didn't convince you that she didn't love you anymore unless you're just a fool," the man firmly stated.

Being a fool might be the case. But hey I'm bigger, stronger and we're in the middle of nowhere and you want to talk to me like that.

Christian looked down with a defeated face. He had to say something to shed light on what really happened.

"Actually at the time that we broke up, I felt like she was confused but that she still loved me."

With a softer tone than before, the man advised Christian, "When you're dealing with love it never gets too late to correct the wrongs of the past. I use to think that you young folks didn't know nothing 'bout love until me and my sweetheart read a poem called 'Love Is' by a young woman from around here 'bout your age. I can't remember her name but she writes a lot of different things but you need to get your hands on that poem and get your hands on the gal that you're in love with. And soon."

"But there's just one problem."

"What's that?"

"I didn't come home to win her back. I came back for her mama's funeral."

"Well that's not a problem. It's an opportunity. If she still loves you, she'll cleave to you now. But don't talk to her about the past right now. That would be low. This is your way of planting your feet and fighting for her by being here for her when she needs you the most despite your past. It makes you look like a real fine man that'll be there no matter what."

"But what if she's using me only because of the grief?"

"Time will tell. But chances are she's not. How do you know she's not grieving letting you go on top of her loss. That's why you can't bring it up but play it cool as if it does not bother you. She needs you now."

"Just like your wife needs you now." Christian looked over to the woman who had completed her set up. "Thank you so much."

"Well hopefully the next time that you come out here, you won't be alone but working on them 50 years. Don't forget the key ingredient is love. Love must come first, be in the middle, and bring up the rear. Get your hands on that poem because to come from a young woman it taught this old fool a thing or two."

With that, Christian shook the man's hand and waved to his wife. As he disappeared into the opening that he had come through, he looked back to see them together. He made up his mind that he would fight to his last breath for Kenali.

When he opened the door to his hotel room, he bent over to pick up a note from the floor.

> *I am here for you. Call me. I'm in room 606.*
> *Love, Julia*

Christian now knew the mysterious woman was actually Julia. He immediately questioned her motives. Still looking at the note, he entered into a true state of discombobulation. He wondered how she could be here to support him when he was here to support Kenali. The mere thought vexed him to the point that he crumpled the paper in his hand tightly. As he threw the note into the wastebasket, he decided that he was not going to deal with her right now. He had an advantage over her and that was knowing his way around.

Once he had quickly grabbed some stuff from his luggage, he went right back out the door. When he turned to check to make sure the door had closed securely behind him, he received a feeling of being watched. For some reason, Christian looked at the peephole on his room door as if it were the culprit. He thought that if Julia was crazy enough to come to Alabama then maybe she was crazy enough to be watching him. Looking to his right and then to his left, seeing no one, he walked slowly down the hallway still being plagued by the feeling of being watched.

When he reached his car, he decided he needed to go shoot the breeze with his cousin Lane until he could figure out what to do about Kenali and Julia. Kenali it was clearcut what he was going to do. But Julia was the monkey that had been thrown in the wrench that he could not predict. One thing was for sure, he would fight hard to keep Julia from messing things up for him with Kenali.

The phone had been ringing off the hook all day. They all had been taking turns answering it. The slew of calls that came in was from family and friends calling to check up on them to see how they were doing. Even though it was a nice gesture, it was overwhelming. However, it was better than entertaining a house full of people again today.

"We're going to turn the ringer off and let the machine catch the rest of them," their daddy said.

He shook his head at the idea of the phone continually ringing into the night. He had never been one to talk on the phone much. He was accustomed to watching his wife talk for hours with different people. It never seemed to wear her out. But the phone calls today were as much as he could take.

"I second that," Kenali said with hand raised.

"Me too. This is a bit much. I know people are concerned but when do we get a moment to rest," Simbol interjected. "And if that fast old gold digger Beatrice call here one mo' time, she's gonna get told off. Enough said," Simbol ranted.

"She needs to quit her mess," Kenali said turning her nose up. "Daddy, who is she anyway?" Kenali further questioned.

Before answering, he paused since he felt a little nervous about explaining who she was.

"Umm. One of your mama's classmates."

"Did she ever try you before now?" Simbol boldly asked without even blinking twice.

Mr. King straightened his back from the question. He cleared his throat. Before he could answer, Simbol started talking again.

"She just seems like one of those women that would love to trap a man especially a married one," Simbol went on and on.

"Yeah and she seemed to be skilled. Knowing exactly how to play on your senses," Kenali replied not happy at all.

"You know these ol' street women don't care nothing about nobody but themselves and what they could beat you out of," Mr. King explained.

He had talked about this long enough and wanted to find a way to change the subject.

"I saw you and Christian out walking. Then you were running across the field wide open. Was everything alright?"

"Oh," Kenali responded with embarrassment, "everything was alright. I just needed to run."

"Girl, you keep running in this heat you will be on the ground somewhere," Simbol added.

"They still young. The heat don't affect them like it does others."

"I hope I wasn't included in the *others*. I'm still young too, Daddy." Simbol looked offended.

Mr. King looked at Simbol then at Kenali not wanting to respond. He knew all too well how easily offended that Simbol could get.

"Daddy, you know how Simbol is. So just walk out the room without saying anything and she'll forget about it soon," Kenali giggled.

Following his youngest daughter's advice, Mr. King got up and walked out the room silently. Kenali began to laugh. Simbol's mouth flew open.

"I was right here in the room when she said it. Daddy? Daddy!" Simbol was shocked. "Kenali, that's not funny and I'm not old."

Kenali continued laughing at the look on Simbol's face.

"Why do you have a complex about being old?"

"I don't have a complex," Simbol pouted. "I was just the baby girl until you came along."

Kenali had heard this spill so much that she mouthed along while Simbol said it. When she finished, Kenali shook her head and planned to do just like her dad until Simbol made a statement to stop her in her tracks.

"There's something to this Beatrice character. I can feel it in my bones and I've never been wrong."

Kenali spun around.

"What do you mean?" Kenali searched the tone of Simbol's voice.

"I mean did you see how nervous Daddy got when I mentioned her name? Even yesterday, he seemed to have been trying extra hard to avoid her."

"So what are you implying, Simbol? That Daddy had something going on with Beatrice?" Kenali didn't like what her sister was getting to.

"No, I'm trying to say that something isn't right but I can't put my finger on it." Simbol twisted her mouth with her thought. "It's like maybe they got too close one time. I don't know. I'm tripping." Simbol waved her hand through the air as if to knock that disgusting thought away.

"Well, I hope you are just tripping. There's no way that dad has stepped out on mom especially with someone who is so disrespectful to come to the house after the funeral."

"All I know is she better not come back around here while I'm here cause I will get to the bottom of it." Simbol peered off into the distance.

Mr. King hung to the corner of the door listening as his two daughters were suspecting something was going on. His heart pounded in his chest. He had to find a way to solve the problem before it flared up any more than it already had.

"Give me yo' wallet!" Lane heard yelled at him from behind with something hard pressing into his back. He attempted to not panic but continued to pump the gas.

"I have something better than that," Lane replied with boldness.

"Oh yeah! What's that?"

"Jesus," Lane was calm.

"Ok. Keep the wallet and give me a ride to church then."

Lane swung around as if he had somehow converted a criminal. When he looked into Christian's face, his shock dissipated.

"Man, you thought you had done something didn't you," Christian laughed.

"Just be glad that I didn't lay hands on you in the name of Jesus and in the name of knocking you out."

"I'm glad that you didn't spray me with gas."

"I should've set yo' butt on fire for playing with me."

Lane and Christian embraced pounding each other on the back. It had been awhile since these cousins had been face-to-face.

"I saw you at the funeral being all chivalrous and stuff."

"You were there? I didn't see you," Christian replied trying to rescan the crowd in his head.

"I know you didn't cause you were *attending* to Ms. King," Lane smirked. "I should have been where you were."

Christian snapped his head back in disbelief of what his cousin was saying. Lane knew better than anyone that Christian had never gotten over Kenali. In the past, Lane had even advised him to get over her and move on. So was this why?

"Man, before your nostrils spread anymore than they already have, I wasn't talking about with Kenali. I was talking about with Simbol. You know us cousins have a thing for them King women."

Christian regained his composure remembering that Lane had developed a thing for Simbol. The nickname Christian had given her of Ms. Sassy always seemed to drive her absolutely nuts even though it perfectly fit her personality.

"Yeah and them King women are a handful," Christian shook off the thought.

Lane suppressed a wrongful thought with a snicker.

"I can imagine," he replied. "Are you still going through with Kenali? Why aren't you there with her now anyway?"

"I had to do some other stuff plus I was coming by to see you real quick."

"Alright, I'm headed home now. Maybe I can take you to the hoops for old time sake."

"Hey if you're not tired of being spanked, I don't mind."

"Man, you ain't never beat me. Ever. Ever!" Lane debated.

Getting into their separate cars, the competition turned to see who would get out of the parking lot first. Their competiveness still carried on well into adulthood. Lane arrived at his house first since he had the more powerful ride, Cadillac Escalade, whereas Christian had his rental car.

"You knew you weren't going to beat me riding in that granny car," Lane jumped out the car with jokes.

"It's a rental!" Christian defended himself. "It's a whole lot better than a thumb and a prayer."

"Yeah, yeah, yeah. I hope you not wearing your granny panties on the court cause I ain't hearing no excuses about you being stiff. Suck it up and get you some Bengay."

"You know what? Other people that got saved are so much milder than you," Christian mocked.

"God knew I was a thug when he converted me. I'm like Peter and Paul. We didn't play before and we still don't now," Lane laughed. Then he tossed the ball at Christian hard. "You can have the ball first cause it don't even much matter."

"Ok. Let me shut that trash talking down," Christian got more serious in his tone.

The two men played ball hard not slacking on one another in any kind of way. Their shirts had long found a spot on the ground since they didn't want anything being a hindrance.

Sweat and muscles flexing was all the teenage girls that lived next door giggled about as they watched the men on the sly. Lane had already had a run in with one of them in which he threatened to take a belt to her backside for being so young trying to talk to him. His conversion from a past of pushing drugs and occasionally pimping a woman here and there wouldn't allow him to let that young girl to set herself up for that type of lifestyle.

"Game! Woohooo. I told you, bruh," Lane cheered violently.

Christian just stood with his hands on his hips shaking his head from side to side breathing heavily. "Dang. I can't believe I let you get the best of me like that. It was a good game though."

"Yeah it was. Let's go in the house. I'm thirsty like a mug," Lane expressed with a big exhale.

Lane reached into the refrigerator pulling out two Powerades tossing one across to Christian. Both men chugged the cold sports drinks as if it was the best thing they ever had. It was refreshing after battling for bragging rights in the hot 3 o'clock sun.

Lane threw his bottle into the trash. "You need anything else?"

Gulping the last of his drink to do likewise with his bottle, Christian replied, "I'm good."

The two cousins went into the den and both fell out on the couch. This was familiar to Christian.

"So when did you get the new set of wheels? That's a clean ride."

"Thanks man. About 6 months ago. What kind of ride are you styling in New York?"

"Camaro drop top."

"That's a nice car and fast. A really big change from that car you had when you were here."

"Do you think that I'm crazy for still loving her?" Christian rushed his words out.

"Yeah. You shouldn't hold that kind of attachment to an old dilapidated car especially when you riding better now," Lane winced at the comparison of Christian's old car to a Camaro.

"I'm not talking about a car. I'm talking about Kenali."

"Umm. Ya gotta let me know when you switch subjects. I was wondering why you attached to an ol' raggedy car that eventually said that it didn't love you anymore."

"Oh, no," Christian gratefully exclaimed. "It's easier to get over a car than a woman. Since I've been here, man, I really want her back."

Lane thought for a moment. "What's the problem? Go get her."

Christian blew his breath in disgust. "Easier said than done. By the way, have you seen her with anyone since I've been gone?"

Lane thought very carefully. "Well it's this one dude."

Christian straightened from his slouched position. Had he been a lighter complexion, he would have flushed red.

"If you could see the look on your face," Lane teased. "Actually, I don't see Kenali that much. I see her mom and pop at church all the time."

"Kenali isn't going to church regularly?" Christian sounded perturbed.

"I didn't say that. She travels a lot."

"Oh. Just checking. She dumped me cause I wasn't in the church."

"Once again. What's the problem? If you love this woman this much and you know what the solution is then why ain't you digging into finding out more about what she's into? I'm just saying. You sure you love her like you say you do?"

Christian hesitated to think on what Lane had said. He had spent the last few years being angry at God for stealing his woman instead of asking how he could have her back.

"I can't answer that. That made a lot of sense."

"Of course it did. I didn't smoke my product. I sold it to people that did," replied Lane wittily.

Christian laughed shaking his head. "So how did you quit selling cold turkey?"

"I didn't."

"What do you mean you didn't?

"I mean it wasn't cold turkey. When the same thing keeps coming at you it's just smart to look at it closer."

Christian thought about it for a moment. He almost had it as it related to him. Lane had one point that would drive the message home.

"Remember, Kenali had probably told you more than once that she didn't want to have sex anymore. When you didn't see it, then she had to walk away."

Ding dong. The witch is dead. Christian got it.

Then suddenly an awkward feeling crept over Christian preventing him from wanting to discuss this topic further. He knew that it was going to lead to them talking about the Lord and when Lane talked about that particular subject, he could be very longwinded.

"Not to change the subject or anything but I'm going to Kenali's. You want to come?"

Lane thought about it briefly making his decision based on his dislike of being the third wheel.

"Naw. I think I'm gonna to pass this time."

Christian sensed his reasoning. "You know Ms. Sassy's going to be there," Christian knew how to get his attention.

Lane hesitated. "I don't know. That just don't seem right."

"What doesn't?"

"I mean with you trying to get back together with Kenali and then I'm going wishing that something could kick off between me and Simbol. That seems like taking advantage of a bad situation. I can't do that. It don't feel right."

"Since you put it like that it does look bad but I didn't come down here to get back together with Kenali. I came down to show support."

"Yeah, right," Lane muffled under his breath.

In defense of himself, Christian shrieked, "I did!"

Then he coughed because the words came out too shrill for the depth of his voice.

Lane chuckled, "You sounded like a girl."

"Dang, I know. That hurt too." Christian massaged his throat.

"Man, you better get to going cause I hope you gonna freshen up before you be around anybody. Don't knock the ladies out if you know what I mean."

"You got jokes hunh. I'll see you later."

Christian and Lane slapped their hands together as they always have.

As soon as Christian sat down in the car, the memory that Julia was in town came back to him. One reason being that he had to go back to the hotel to get out his sweat drenched clothes. The second reason was that when he looked at his cell, she had called three times and left a text.

Call me when you get a chance. Love you.

Love you, Christian's thoughts screamed. Where is this coming from? Why are you here? And so many other things were crowding his mind. It got to the point that he dreaded going back to the hotel. He almost pulled back up to Lane's house to borrow some clothes and use his shower but his boxers were drenched with sweat. Borrowing another man's underwear just wasn't his style.

Reluctantly he continued on to the hotel. He attempted to figure out which of the cars in the parking lot belonged to Julia. The majority of them were rentals making it an impossible feat.

Christian went into the lobby with care. He searched the area before he walked into it to see if she was lurking around watching for him. Walking up to the elevator, the bell dinged as it was getting ready to open. He almost sprinted away from it just at the thought that it could be about to reveal Julia. Before he could make a move, the doors parted quickly and to his surprise, no one was in it.

When he got into the elevator, he noticed that every button had been pressed. He was going to have to wonder every time the door opened if she was waiting to get on.

"Stupid kids."

He sighed heavily. Thinking to himself that he was a grown man afraid to come in contact with a lady that couldn't have been any more than 5'7 and 120 pounds soaking wet. He had to rethink his last statement.

"I'm the one that's stupid," Christian paused. "And I'm tripping," he paused again. "And I'm talking to myself in an elevator."

Christian felt relieved to have made it through all the elevator stops without seeing Julia. He let out a deep breath when he closed his room door behind him. He leaned against it in relief. Then he jumped from feeling the vibration of his cell in his pocket.

Have you made it back to your room yet? Let me know. I really want to see you.

"Are you watching me? And why would I care if you wanted to see me? You're not supposed to be here anyway," Christian yelled at the text message before throwing the phone on the bed in anger. All his actions of undressing were in the same manner as he snatched his clothes off.

Julia had a way of aggravating Christian which was the prime reason he broke up with her. She was too smothering. Too clingy. And would never take "no" for an answer. If he even called her or made any contact with her, she would never let him out of her sight.

Christian made up in his mind that he was going to drive her crazy this time by not returning any of her phone calls. The worst she could do, he thought, was to pester him once he got back to New York.

I wonder why Christian isn't returning my calls, were the thoughts of Julia.

Standing in front of her hotel room window looking directly at the rental car that Christian was driving, she saw him get out the car to walk into the hotel. It was then that she sent one of the messages. She couldn't fathom what had him so preoccupied inside his room when he was alone.

Walking away from the window, she sat hopelessly onto the bed allowing herself to fall back. Her light-brown eyes zoomed in on the popcorn ceiling until it drove her cross-eyed.

Closing her eyes, she thought of the times that she and Christian had spent together. They were the happiest times that she ever had with anyone. She knew he loved her so much even though he slipped and called her by another woman's name one of the many times they had made love.

That name was burned into her brain. After reading the obituary from the funeral, she knew exactly who Kenali was. Clearly, Kenali must have begged him to come. Julia was patient as she sat in the very back of the church watching Christian make a fuss of Kenali at the funeral.

However, what Christian and Kenali had was over long ago. After the calling of the wrong name, he reassured her of that by explaining that she had pushed him away, which upset him. Julia of all people could understand that very well.

Every man that she had been with somehow felt the need to cheat on her or push her away from them in time. They would love on her in the beginning falling all over her remarking how beautiful she was. She sported the complexion, eye color and hair texture given to her from her parents being mixed race. However, when she showed a man how much she appreciated him, he would misuse her. Christian was different and she appreciated that about him. That's exactly why she came to the funeral. She knew that Christian was going to need her support to keep Kenali from misusing him.

But she could only do that if he answered the phone. Rolling over to grab her cell from the nightstand, she checked to make sure that she still had a signal. That could be the reason that she hadn't received a phone call from him. He must be having poor reception.

"I'll call his room," Julia beamed with a bright idea.

She crawled across the bed to reach the phone that was on the opposite nightstand. Dialing his room number, twirling the cord of the phone with her finger, she had expectation. After the fifth ring, she figured that he was in the shower since he did look a little sweaty. She hung up and began to think about what she should do next. Julia repeatedly tapped her chin with her index finger staring into space as if the answer would manifest in front of her eyes.

Julia jumped up from the bed quickly. She ran into the bathroom to glance herself over. Everything was in order. She swung the room door open with so much force the hair of her freshly flat-ironed bangs shuffled around on her forehead. She got into the hall speed racing to the elevator. Inside the elevator, she admired her new hairstyle, which in this humidity, took more attention than her naturally curly hair

When she arrived at Christian's room door, she regrouped before knocking. After he didn't answer, she pressed her ear to the door. She didn't hear anything. Then she went downstairs to go out to the parking lot. The spot where he had parked was empty. *That was fast*, she thought.

"He must be going to Kenali's. I got to go save him."

Julia doubled back into her room, grabbing the phonebook. She flipped pages hastily. There wasn't a listing for Kenali King. Then she thought about how she didn't have a home phone either but just used her cell. Scanning over the list of Kings in which there were quite a healthy list of them, she ripped the page out folding and shoving it into her purse. She grabbed her keys and sunglasses heading back out the door.

Julia had always been resourceful and she proved it when she reached the lobby. Spotting the desk attendant watching TV in the lobby, she walked over to start a conversation.

"Hello there. Anything good on?" She flashed a seductive smile at him.

When he noticed her beauty, he sat up straight.

"Hey. Umm. No nothing good's on. Umm did you want to watch the TV," he fumbled over his words.

He offered her the remote. Julia gently pushed his hand back towards him.

She giggled, "No, I can't right now. Besides the day is too beautiful to be inside and it's almost gone."

"Yeah it was or it is or umm yeah," he sheepishly grinned. Her touch rendered him unable to gain his composure.

She flirted with him even though he was not her type. She never had a thing for the thug looking guy, which was evident although he had on a uniform. His posture, cornrows, and the apparent oversized clothing that he had on told his whole story.

"I was wondering if you could help me find someone while there is some daylight still available," she turned the conversation but allowed her overwhelmingly pleasant voice to remain.

"Sure. I'll do what I can."

Julia sat down onto the couch very close to the young man.

"Great. I'll owe you one." She winked at him biting her lower lip passionately. *Why am I doing this*, she thought before she continued. "I'm in town for a funeral and I was trying to find where Kenali King lived so I could drop in to pay my respects."

"Oh ok. I know them. Yeah I can tell you exactly where she lives. But they are meeting at their pop's house."

"Yes, I know but I was going to see if I could catch her at home."

He gave turn-by-turn directions with wonderful descriptions even down to Kenali living in a brick house with a red door. "The only one on the street," he said.

That shouldn't be too hard to find, she thought, *especially if Christian's car is sitting outside.* Which it wasn't when she got there. However, the house was exactly just like the young man said. She giggled at how she unnecessarily flirted information out of him. She didn't have to do it but she needed some attention especially during Christian's hiatus of doing so.

Julia dug into her purse to pull out the page she had ripped from the phone book. She started with the first name on the list.

"Alto King. I recognize that name from the obituary."

She then keyed the address into her GPS. When she was almost there, she began to notice certain landmarks that looked familiar. Her mind began to search why it was so when she realized that she was here yesterday when she had followed at a great distance behind Christian. But it was something else other than being there yesterday. She felt it even then.

"In 1000 feet turn right," the GPS mechanically instructed.

Julia had just begun to wish that the GPS could tell her why this area was so familiar when she saw something that she hadn't seen in years. Today the driving directions included some extra turns that she didn't make yesterday. These turns were painfully rushing back to her mind. Her pulse began to race. Sweat began to form onto Julia's upper lip. Her eyebrows wrinkled dramatically. She pulled the car over onto the side of the road.

She could not believe that she was facing one of the many skeletons that she nailed to the back of the closet. *I can't be here*, she thought gripping the steering wheel increasingly tight. Down the street and on the right, everything from her deeply concealed past screamed at her. She had made a vow never to come back to that house again; not even passing by it.

Looking down at the screen of the GPS, even though she had two more miles before she reached her destination, she couldn't go any further. Julia was paralyzed.

She shook herself making the decision to turn around allowing the GPS to reroute her. She just wasn't ready to go past that one particular house. Not now. Hopefully not ever would she have to.

Now arriving at the house of Alto King, she knew where Christian had hurried off to. There were several cars in the driveway and lining the street.

"They sure do have a lot of company," Julia marveled. Then she compared the amount of visitors at her father's funeral, which totaled five if you counted her and her stepmom. He was always such a horrifically mean man who was impossible to love and his exit showed that others felt the same as she did; he was a pure son of a—.

Her mind released the thoughts of her father when she spotted Christian standing in front of the window. She would know that scrumptious physique anywhere. Now how was she going to get him out of this house? Not even breaking her stare, she began digging in her purse sending her hand on a search for her cell.

She called. He dug into his pocket, looked at his phone, and returned it back to his pocket. Julia was infuriated.

"Stop ignoring me!"

How could Kenali work that fast? Regardless of how good Kenali was, she was going to be better. Kenali was going down just as the sun was doing. After all, Julia had come back to an area that she vowed never to return just to save the man whom she loved.

Christian seems so agitated especially after looking at his phone, Kenali thought. Even after the time apart, she could still read his body language and that quick twitch of his eyebrow meant that something was getting on his nerve.

Was his being here bringing an unbalance somewhere else in his life? Kenali crossed the room to stand beside him. She had to investigate. Besides, the last thing that she wanted to do was to keep opening her mind up to the possibility of them being together again if he was in a relationship.

After arriving by his side, she realized how foolishly she was thinking. *He's here to help you cope.*

"Is everything alright Christian?"

Looking down into her face, he placed a hand of reassurance onto her shoulder. "Everything is just fine." *Or at least it will be when I take care of my uninvited NYC tagalong*, he thought.

"I really appreciate you being here but I would understand if you need to go back."

"Shhhh. Don't say that. I have nothing to go back early for." *Except to put this woman in check*, his thought rambled. "I already told you that I'm here for the week."

"Well ok then. I just didn't want to be holding you here from something," *or someone*, she thought.

Kenali almost wished that Christian heard her thoughts to swear to her that there was no one else. She didn't want her heart tangled in a love triangle.

To clear her head, she looked out the window. She noticed a woman sitting in a car seemingly looking directly at them. It was hard to tell because the sun was almost gone. Kenali dismissed it charging it to someone trying to see the house number making sure they had the correct place. However, she gently touched Christian's arm to pull him from in front of the window. She looked back and the car was pulling off being replaced by another one that she did not want to see—Ms. Beatrice.

Beatrice was walking fast down the walkway towards the front door. This 'ol trick' as Simbol has referred to her, was on a mission. Out of the three women that flaunted themselves in front of their dad, this one was something serious—she wasn't playing. She was determined to get her clutches on their dad. And Kenali was determined to not let this floozy of a woman get next to him.

Kenali swung around getting eye contact with Simbol who was across the room. When their eyes met, they instinctively knew that it was show time.

"Excuse me for a moment, Christian."

Before he could respond, Kenali was almost at the front door with Simbol hot on her trail. She swung the door open with so much force that Beatrice, who was prepared to knock, jumped back startled.

"Hi. Ms. Beatrice, isn't it?

"Yes." Beatrice had not yet retained her composure.

"We appreciate you stopping by but tonight we are just having a gathering of family members. But we'll let everybody know that you stopped by."

"But Alto told me I could come by."

"Alto?" Simbol repeated with disgust forgetting that this woman and her dad were the same age putting them on first name basis.

"Yes. Your father."

"Well he told us otherwise," Kenali interjected trying to sound a little less interrogative.

Simbol who had now stepped in front of Kenali starred impregnably into Beatrice's eyes. Beatrice returned the stare with the same fever.

"Good evening, Beatrice. Come on in," Mr. King said from behind his two daughters.

Kenali looked back at her father and stepped aside but Simbol on the other hand never moved one inch. When Beatrice walked passed her, Simbol with all of her usual boldness let her know what was up.

"I see you devil!"

Beatrice tooted her nose into the air and smiled as if she had the upper hand.

As they watched their dad walk away with this woman by his side, Simbol seethed.

"I don't like that heifer right there. And what kind of control does she have over our dad."

Simbol was so hot that she slammed the door. Had Lane not actually been in the doorway, it would have made such a loud noise that it would have captured everyone's attention.

"Oh, hey Lane. We're so sorry. Are you alright?" Kenali was super apologetic.

"I—I didn't see you," Simbol stuttered.

"No problem. But you got a good arm on you. I know not to make you mad," Lane flashed a boyish smile at Simbol making eye contact the entire time. His look softened Simbol in a way that she didn't want it to. She looked away. He continued. "Now I know why my cuz calls you Ms. Sassy."

Simbol was jolted from her softer persona. She gasped in disbelief. "I haven't heard that in years." Simbol then shot a cold look at Christian who was approaching the threesome standing in the doorway.

Clueless to the comment, he changed his approach to one of caution. "What did I do to deserve that look?"

"You know what you did."

"You gotta help me out. I'm totally clueless, Ms. Sassy."

Simbol sucked her teeth walking off dramatically.

Kenali gently tapped Christian in his chest. "Why do you do my sis like that?"

"It's so much fun. You should try it but what did I do?"

Kenali shook her head smiling. "Let me go calm her down."

"Kenali, remember she was already ticked off before I got here. We just added a lil gas to the fire," Lane joked with his deep scruffy yet seductive voice.

The two men watched Kenali walk away in search of Simbol.

"I thought you weren't coming."

"I changed my mind. I didn't have nothing else to do."

"Alright. I was sitting over here. Come on."

Kenali found Simbol outside on the back porch. Before she walked out the house, she saw her dad sitting in the family room. Beatrice was sitting across from him. Thankfully, they weren't sitting side-by-side and the room was filled with other people with the main one being Divine who just had such an awesome craft of nicely getting next to people that she didn't like.

"Why did you storm off like that?"

"Girl, he was getting to me?"

"Who? Christian? He didn't mean—"

"No. Lane. That man is sexy. Child, I had a hot flash"

Kenali jerked back not expecting none of those words to come out her sister's mouth.

"You got a thing for Lane? I thought you didn't like Lane?"

"I didn't like any man then because I had been damaged by one. That doesn't make me a lesbian like that so called counselor that told you to let your good man go. Now that he's here, do you regret it?"

Kenali remembered trying to do the right thing by seeking Christian counseling when she kept falling into bed with Christian. Even though she knew that the info didn't feel right, she carried out every word; she broke up with Christian so that they wouldn't be unequally yoked which was the phrase that the counselor used very convincingly.

"I regret every bit of it."

"Mama would be so proud to see him here."

"Yes, she would be."

The sisters sat quietly in the dark with nothing but a little light from a moon that wasn't fully exalted. They each heard the sniffles of the other knowing exactly what was going on. Then Simbol cleared her throat.

"I don't trust Beatrice. It's something about that lady that's all wrong. That 'ol trick got something up her sleeve."

"Simbol, I feel the same way too. The other ladies seemed harmless but she feels eerie."

"I know." Sitting back in her chair surrounded by night, Simbol peered into the family room unnoticed by anyone. She stealthily watched Beatrice carry on conversation as if she was familiar with everyone in the room. Simbol could not and would not let this go. "Trust me, I know."

As Mr. King closed the door behind the last departing guest, he sighed with relief. He then saw Divine tidying the place up. When he continued his search, he didn't see his other two daughters.

"You don't have to do this tonight. We'll get it in the morning."

"I don't mind. Besides, I'm hoping the boys will let me sleep a little late tomorrow."

"If you insist. I know it doesn't do any good to keep trying to talk you out of it. You're just like your mama." He put his arm around Divine squeezing her shoulder. "Where are them sisters of yours?"

"I believe they're outside with Christian and Lane. You need me to get them?"

"Yes, but I need you to get them straight."

Divine stopped busying herself with cleaning off the coffee table. She stood up straight. "What do you mean, Daddy?"

"I mean they can be mean as two snakes when they touch and agree on something. They don't know how to kill people with kindness like you do. You get what I'm saying."

"Kind of. What happened?"

Mr. King exhaled loudly. "Well, I saw they had Beatrice hemmed up at the front door. They had no intentions of letting her in. I'm not sure but I think Simbol called the woman a devil."

Divine burst into laughter. "I'm sorry. I didn't mean to laugh but that sounds exactly like Simbol."

"I know but she doesn't have to act like that when people are coming to be hospitable."

"I'll try to talk to her to see if that helps any but you know she's bold with a touch of craziness plus she's set in her ways."

"I know. That girl has always been like that even when she was a child. She was always bucking her eyes at people and she still does it now. I swear your mama dropped her on her head."

"Who got dropped on their head, Daddy?" Simbol questioned.

Mr. King and Divine just stood looking at her wondering when she came into the room.

"Are you all enjoying playing spades?" Divine quickly changed the subject.

"Whenever the subject is changed that means that you were the subject." Simbol was halfway joking but when she looked back and forth between them both, she turned serious. "I can't believe y'all was talking about me."

"Simbol, sweetie," Divine started softly, "we weren't talking about you in a bad way. Dad just wanted me to talk to you and Kenali about some things."

"Things? Things like what?" Simbol was now dry and short with her words. She already had the feeling that this was about her least favorite person in the world—Beatrice.

"What I told her to talk to y'all about is being a little nicer to people especially when they are coming around paying a visit."

"I bet this has something to do with that Beatrice!" Simbol's tone was excruciatingly sharp.

"You better watch your tone towards me. I know you're grown but I'm still your father."

Simbol already knew better. She can't believe that she let the mentioning of that woman get the best of her forcing her to move out of character towards her dad. "I'm sorry. I didn't mean to say it like that."

"Apology accepted. What do you have against Beatrice anyway?"

"I can see what she's up to. We all see it."

"And what's that?"

"She's trying to get next to you. Mama just died!" Simbol's tears were streaming hot down her face now. "And she thinks she's going to come in here and take Mama's place."

Mr. King got closer to his daughter to hold her. Divine turned her back to cry privately.

"I'm going to introduce you to her so that she can tell you who she really is. She and your mother were best friends all of their lives until she moved to Mississippi when you kids were little. They talked on the phone at least twice a month for hours running up the phone bill."

Kenali, who had entered the room quietly when she saw things getting heated, covered her mouth to keep from crying aloud. How could they have made such a mistake? That would make her second one counting Ms. Vera.

"Daddy, we're sorry. We were just trying to protect you."

"I know baby girl but I already told y'all that I have been around long enough to know the character of people. Some can hide it pretty good but some you can see them coming a mile away. I loved your mama and I would not disrespect her like this."

❧ ❧

All three ladies embraced their father as he tried to embrace them all at the same time. They hugged and cried until each of them got what they needed.

Sitting in her car with the lights off parked underneath the row of trees that lined the street, she could see the family hug that was taking place. She turned the corners of her mouth down in disgust.

"Honey, you're going to pay for calling me a devil," Beatrice loathed. "Even if you are right."

"I can't believe that she had the nerve to stare at me!" Julia heatedly paced the floor of her hotel room. "Christian just let her touch all over him and lead him around like some kind of little puppy." Julia continued her venting. "He's so stupid for not recognizing what Kenali is doing! Can't he realize I'm here to help him!"

Julia's anger was getting the best of her. She stormed into the bathroom looking into the mirror seeing her face flushed red. Her lighter skin complexion had become tinted by her emotions, which were through the roof. She needed to take her frustrations out on something. The complimentary soaps, shampoo and lotion that sat on the countertop would have to suffice for right now. She backhanded them with exceeding joy.

When they landed into the tub, the nanosecond of satisfaction dissipated. She needed something else more pleasing. Kenali would be the perfect solution. Then her mind flashed back to the house she fled from earlier. *Maybe something there could do the trick or at least it used to*, her mind beckoned her to revisit that place.

"No!" she screamed at her reflection in the mirror. "You already beat that," through clinched teeth, she motivated herself to stay away from the past.

She needed something to take her mind away from those feelings. The urge was getting stronger and stronger as it was feeding off her current emotions of feeling out of control.

Before the desire to delve into the past could take over completely, she hastily went to her purse, which was on the bed, falling to her knees frantically digging for her phone.

"I just need to call someone that's all."

She dialed the number faster than speed dial; she was in a hard place. The person answered the phone, as they were half-asleep. Not considering the time being an hour ahead of where she was, making it 1:15a.m. in New York.

"Hello," a groggy female voice came over the phone.

Julia didn't say anything. She scrambled to gather her words knowing all too well the warning her friend had given her about coming to Alabama. Since Julia had awakened her, she felt an 'I told you so' coming which was the last thing she needed to hear right now.

The pause was so long that her friend had to announce again she had received the call. This time her voice was clearer.

"Julia, are you there? Is everything alright?"

Tears crawled from her eyes as she forced her mouth shut so tightly it hurt.

"Yes. I'm here," she managed to whimper not wanting to say what she really needed to.

"Girl, what's wrong with you? You don't sound ok. Is this about Christian?" Concern was blaring through the phone.

Julia already knew of the one person in the world that she could tell anything to and it was her true friend on the other end of the phone. This woman was there for Julia whenever she needed an encouraging word or a shoulder to cry on. They had been through the program together which was where they met.

"I'll take your silence to mean that it's about Christian and that he's done something to you to make you think about doing something so crazy even though you know how hard it was for you to kick that habit."

Her friend knew the inside of addiction to the point that Julia didn't have to say a word. "Well, let me tell you like this, Christian or anybody else is not worth losing a five year staying clean streak. You get high this one time and you're going to feel awful. And then you're going to have to start all over again. Take it from me, that's a hell you don't want to live in."

Julia sighed. She knew that her friend was right. This situation wasn't worth going back to the life on drugs always wondering how she was going to get her next fix especially when the bank account had already been cleaned out.

"Thanks. I'm sorry for waking you up but I really needed you tonight."

"Anytime. You know you're my girl and we can't let each other down," she paused thinking carefully on her next words. "Julia, please come home. Just go to the airport in the morning and catch the first flight this way."

"Are you trying to tell me that you told me not to come here in the first place?" Julia sounded slightly yet noticeably agitated.

"No. I would never say that."

"Even if it's what you meant?"

"That's not what I'm saying at all. I'm being your friend and you're too far away for me to help you instantly. Besides, there aren't any people on your side down there. You don't have anymore family that live in the area."

Julia's mind reverted to feeling as if Kenali has won. If there was one thing about Julia that was her strongest asset, that would be her determination to get her way. And she was going to get it here in Alabama. She was feeling empowered all over again. Even better now that the taste of drugs had been replaced with pure competition.

"Thanks, lady, but I'm going to be alright. I'm on a mission." Julia smiled which increased the more her newfound thoughts of how she would stand victorious entered her head. "Don't worry about me. I can't lose."

"**K**en, we beat 'em girl!" Christian exclaimed at his and Kenali's current Spades victory over Simbol and Lane.

"Tag team back again," Kenali sang as she stood up to reach across the table to give Christian a high five.

Lane blocked it by pushing their hands out the air. "Naw. It ain't even going down like that. Y'all didn't win but one game the whole night and you wanna stunt like that? Nope!"

"I know that's right, Lane. We got tired of beating them a long time ago. And they want to dance and sing like they did something. That's a joke," Simbol sarcastically laughed.

Lane and Simbol then stood up mimicking the charades of Christian and Kenali in a comical way. They high fived each other missing hands while singing the same song.

"Christian, somebody got jokes. When you look at the scores, you beat us 2 games to 1 and each game was only by 10 points at the most," Kenali defended.

"It don't even much matter. A win is a win, boo," Lane included.

Lane enjoyed having people to interact with on this level. He and Christian had never hung around much since

Lane had been saved. He was a whole lot freer since he gave his life to the Lord than when he was selling drugs. He used to be one of those mellow, laid-back guys that sat and observed never talking much. His money was on his mind. His mind was on someone crossing into his territory. Now his mind was on the peace that God provided. He now slept well every night.

He was thankful that Christian wanted him to come by. Had he not changed his mind, he would have never gotten to see Simbol nor be of some help with taking their minds off the current situation. He didn't know what it meant to lose someone to that degree but he remembered when his aunt, Christian's mom passed, and how that grief had those times in which it would come in to hold Christian hostage without warning.

So tonight, he thought Christian was trying to pull a hook up but he used his past experience to cater to the best interest of these ladies.

"Well y'all. It's late. So I'm gonna head out. Got to get up early to handle my business."

"Ok, Lane. I'm glad you came by to help me beat these amateurs."

"It was my pleasure, Ms. Sassy," he grinned. "Sorry but I couldn't resist it. But next time you want me to come by to help you Spade spank them again, just give me a holla."

Christian and Kenali looked at each other realizing that Simbol and Lane was actually a perfect match. They both were trash talkers.

"Yeah whatever," Kenali waved them off with her hand pretending to be disgusted. "Simbol don't you want to walk Lane out so you guys can finish your gloating on the way to the door." Kenali had other intentions behind her suggestion based on their earlier conversation.

Just from the mentioning of it, Simbol suddenly got nervous. For some reason, she looked at the walk through the house as them being alone. What was she going to say? How was she going to act? This was easier when she had cards in her hands. So many thoughts raced through her mind.

"Yeah. We'll take our victory stroll," Lane included as his last comment on their winning for the night. He then turned putting his hand into the center of Simbol's back while opening the door to the house with the other. "Ladies first."

Simbol walked into the house stiff as a board acting like a schoolgirl on a date with her first crush. *Girl, get it together. You are grown. Why are you acting like this?* She scorned herself.

The last time she could remember a man touching her was when her ex was slapping her around. Nothing gentle like this, which was surprising for Lane's character. He had this seemingly thuggish, bad boy side but the way he softly looked at her made her melt. She couldn't even speak correctly when he looked that way.

She sped up to get to the front door before she fell apart.

"Well, here we are again. I just hope you won't slam the door in my face this time," Lane flashed another heart-melting smile.

Simbol wished that she could shut the door in his face to spare her of the embarrassment of being socially retarded. She didn't know how to carry on a conversation with him without it being in a group setting.

Tell him you won't close the door on him, she thought.

"I won't close the door on you this time. And I can't apologize enough for that."

"Don't mention it. I understand that you just gotta act up every now and then."

"Oh that's what you call it?"

"Yep. I sure do." Lane paused. "So whatcha got going on in the morning?"

Simbol thought briefly not being able to think of anything. She was totally out of her normal element. "Nothing I guess. What about you? I know you said that you have to handle some business."

Lane chuckled. "I was talking about Kingdom business. I teach the children's Sunday School class at church."

Simbol joined in with his laughter. This was becoming easier than she thought it would be. "Oh that's awesome. I totally didn't see that coming. So what church do you go to?"

"Cornerstone of Life. The same church your mom and pop goes to."

Lane felt awkward talking about Mrs. King. She was a good woman who would not let anyone pass any judgment on him for his appearance or actions. She always told him that, "If you're not being yourself, when God calls roll, He won't recognize you when you show up."

Simbol swallowed the tears that were trying to come up. She wondered how long the feeling would last to become teary eyed whenever her mom was mentioned.

Shaking it off to speak, "Great. I'll see you at church then. I can't wait to see how you handle your business." She smiled extra wide and he did the same.

They said their goodbyes. Lane walked to his car while Simbol slowly closed the door following him with her eyes. As far as she could tell, Lane was everything that she needed. He definitely was what she wanted, not too soft but with the right amount of rough edges to keep her attention.

As for Lane, he was one happy man. He was thankful he had reached a point to be able to approach a nice woman like Simbol not having to hide his past street life. It all made everything he went through worth it just to be able to do a recap of the night in his head on his drive home. God was certainly good to him. Favor wasn't fair but he was glad it was over his life.

Kenali looked across the table at Christian now that they were all alone. A good feeling was overcoming her to the point she almost wanted to act towards him as she did when they were still together. She wanted to kiss him. Shaking the thought from her head, she just knew her feelings were due to the late time.

"It's after midnight," Kenali shrieked after looking at the clock on her cell phone.

"Wow. This night flew by."

"Yes, it did," she agreed. "I really want to thank you guys for coming by. It did me a world of good and I know it was the same for Simbol."

"Don't mention it. Anything we can do to help."

Christian felt as he had gotten the same amount of benefit out of their time together as the ladies did. He was able to spend some time with his cousin who was a whole lot better now. Lane was actually fun to hang around. But most importantly, he was able to hang around the woman that he never stopped loving.

Kenali had a flash of thought. "Oh wow. I keep getting my days mixed up. It's actually Sunday. Lane was talking about church when he said he had some business to handle."

"Are you going?"

Kenali pondered if she could handle going to church this soon after the funeral. "I'm not sure. I need to go to keep my strength up but I'm going to have to play this one by ear." Kenali juggled the thoughts of going and not going to church in her mind. She was leaning increasingly towards going so that she could apologize to Ms. Vera while she was there. "What about you? Are you going?"

Christian readjusted himself in his seat. He hadn't been to church in years until he came to the funeral. "No. Not this time. I have some other things that I have to take care of." He made a quick list in his head just in case she asked what it was.

"Ok. I can understand that you're trying to squeeze a bunch of stuff into the short time you're going to be here."

Even though Kenali understood, her mind questioned if Christian had gotten saved or even thought of the possibility. Then again, why would he since she pushed him away so harshly. Why would he want to serve a God like the one she terribly misrepresented?

"Yeah. And on that note, I'm going to head out so that you can get some sleep." Christian stood walking around to her side of the table. He hugged her planting a gentle kiss on the side of her face. "Call me if you need anything," he lowered his voice then he released her.

Kenali so greatly missed his touch. She made a poor attempt at not indulging in the moment by allowing her flesh to savor the feeling of his lips on her face. It longed for more of the feeling of his hot breath, which caressed her ear as he spoke into it.

Oh, Jesus, she thought. Her hormones mixed with grief were turning against her. Although she felt as if she was wearing her thoughts on her face, they went completely unnoticed.

"Thanks. You being here means a lot to me. To all of us. We appreciate you."

They walked through the house that had no signs of anyone being downstairs. She thought of how her dad must have long been retreated to upstairs. But where did Simbol disappear to that fast?

When she opened the front door to let Christian out, she patted him gently on the side of his bicep as he passed by. That proved to be a big mistake; she felt the masculinity in his arms. Something that she hadn't felt in years jolted down her spine.

"Jesus," slipped out her mouth.

Christian turned around to face her. "What was that?"

Having to think fast on her feet, "I said see ya."

He turned waving his hand goodbye. Before long, he had entered into his car disappearing into the night.

Kenali then scurried around the bottom floor of the house to see if Simbol was somewhere downstairs. She found her in the kitchen eating ice cream from the carton. That was the first sign that something heavy was on her mind.

"Tell me all about it and give me a spoon too."

"It's already right here." Simbol pointed her spoon in the direction of where she had set a place at the countertop for Kenali.

Kenali straddled the bar stool like a little kid. "We're in trouble."

"You ain't never lied," Simbol quickly agreed. "I thought certain places in my heart were dead until tonight."

Kenali just nodded slowly in agreement spooning ice cream into her mouth.

"Kenali, Mama just died and I feel so guilty about having these feelings arise. I kind of feel like we're supposed to be grieving and not playing card games and connecting as if nothing has happened. Then the other side of me says that our mama is smiling down on us for still trying to live."

"I feel the same way. So conflicted on the inside. My hormones are acting up and the same heart is crying and rejoicing. I feel like a total mess. So I'm definitely going to church in the morning to get a right now word."

"Yes, Lord," Simbol cosigned with her sister.

Kenali looked around the kitchen where her mom had spent a lot of time prepping meals and dishing out healing conversations. They desperately needed one of those moments right here, right now in the King's kitchen.

Sitting outside in the driveway of the place that he called home from the time he was 8 or so, Christian's most prized memories flooded him. The times that he and Lane played tackle football on the front lawn. One of those times, they got too rough, leading to Lane losing a tooth before it was time for the Tooth Fairy. Then there was the time when his mom sprayed an unsuspecting bike riding Christian with the hosepipe. That was the good old days that sometimes he longed for now.

The light from the living room lamp glowed giving the appearance that someone still lived here. He almost thought about staying here while he was in town but he knew that it needed a good dusting first.

After his mom died, he did in fact move back in until he left for NYC. Lane had been good about coming by to check on the place twice a month while Christian sent a check once a year to cover the small utility usage.

Here it was, almost 1a.m. when he cracked the seal of the door. Everything was just as it was the day he left in a confused rage. The picture of Kenali in the living room was still face down from when he slammed it. He reached to pick it up realizing the frame had been shattered. He laughed from the remembrance of his drunken solo pity party, which caused him to take his frustrations out on the frame.

The more he walked, the more memories he had of his mom and him. It would have been great if he had more memories of his father but he *wasn't that kind of dad* as he remembering him saying one Christmas Eve to his mom through the door. He didn't even have the nerve to come in to face a 12-year old that he was breaking yet another promise to. By the time Christian reached 13, he no longer needed a dad. He became the man of the house taking care of his favorite girl who was there for him as a mother and a father.

Christian walked into her bedroom, which he had not disturbed; leaving it just as she had. He walked to the side of the bed that she slept on. When he sat, it creaked. His mom loved antiques and therefore her whole room was vintage. From the white skinny post bed that he always joked he had seen in a horror movie to the white dressers with the rustic antique knobs. Even her wicker rocker *was a great bargain at an antique sale,* she beamed to a 15-year old Christian who thought that it was just old and ugly.

His mom's favorite picture still sat upright on the nightstand displaying a happy Christian and Kenali. Had drunkenness not lead him to pass out those years ago he would have come to destroy this one also. Well maybe not since he was on it.

"Mom, you always did think we were going to get married."

Now he opened the drawer, reached down into its deepness and pulled out a little black box. It had a pop to it when it opened. The princess cut diamond ring was still in it. He was going to propose to Kenali had they not had life changing surprises for each other on the same day. He thought about taking it back to the store but he was too hurt. Therefore, he left it with his mom's memory of what was good.

"Mom, she broke my heart but for some reason I still got hope."

Christian returned the box back to its resting place. Walking across the room, he opened the blinds. Then he sat into the wicker rocker. It may have been old but it was always comfortable even though he never admitted it. His mom probably knew because every time, which was often, he came to hang out in her room, his rear end found its way into this chair.

Now he sat rocking looking out the window in the comfort of the past until he fell asleep.

The vibration of Christian's phone in his pocket caused him to jump. When he opened his eyes, the sun brightly greeted him.

"What time is it?" He cleared his groggy throat. Looking at his watch, he had to squint since his eyes hadn't adjusted to being open. "Whoa. It's 9 o'clock?" Christian jolted from the rocking chair leaving it swaying violently.

As he ran into the bathroom to relieve himself, he tilted his stiffened neck from side-to-side. Then he checked his phone. It was Julia calling—again. He had so many missed calls from her that he was beginning to think that she was really crazy or something was wrong with her memory. Even while he was holding the phone looking at the missed calls that came back-to-back, she sent him yet another text message.

Come to the hotel. I have a surprise for you!

Once again, Christian dismissed her messages. "I don't like surprises!" he yelled. Julia was one of the primary reasons that Christian couldn't lay his religious differences to the side to go to church with Kenali today. It was all because he saw Julia sitting outside Mr. King's house yesterday like some kind of stalker. He had to be sure to handle this psycho woman today.

He walked into the kitchen to get something to drink. Having to wash the glass first gave him a little more time to think how he was going to get Julia to go back to New York before she messed things up with Kenali. With only a slim chance, the last thing he needed is for Julia to cut that in half. Besides, Kenali was grieving and didn't need those little childish games Julia played to multiply her sorrow.

Julia had tried this stunt once before in New York six months after they had broken up. She attempted to cause trouble for the new lady at work that had been hired to be Christian's assistant. The threatening looks Julia flashed to her and the bumping into her repeatedly while sucking her teeth only aggravated something this woman had already experienced. By the time Julia got finished with this lady, the lady lost her job. She slapped Julia so hard, Christian swore he saw her taste buds hit the floor and run. On the inside, he applauded her.

Julia however took off for a week due to all the teasing. Flyers were created about learning self-defense, padded helmets and the list went on and on. Needless to say, Julia was never really liked around the office once people got to know her. In the beginning, she comes off as a person who is helpful and very nice but the real Julia comes out after a couple of months. You then see the clingy, needs constant attention, aggravating control freak who blames others for everything that happens to her.

Christian gulped the water down hard cringing just by thinking about Julia. The only good thing he could say about her was that she had a banging body. Nevertheless, a knock out body with horrible personality traits just wasn't enough. Moreover, being raised by a single mom who schooled him to look past the flesh. His mom would tell him all the time to look past the body to see a woman with his mind not his eyes.

Getting ready to walk out the door heading to the hotel, Christian took note that everything was off. He saw the timers that Lane had placed on various lamps in a couple of rooms. Nodding his head in approval, he locked the door, checked the time, and calculated how much time he had to rid Alabama of Julia before Kenali and the others got out of church at 12.

Meet me at the hotel in one hour. I need to talk to you.

Christian sent a quick text setting their meeting in motion, which gave him an hour to grab a bite to eat. He just couldn't deal with Julia on an empty stomach.

Pulling up to the neighborhood diner that had the best chicken and waffles he had ever tasted, he salivated from memory. He wished very often that this family owned establishment had a branch in New York.

Christian walked to the back, seating himself in a corner booth. He and Kenali always liked to sit in this particular spot to look out over the lake.

The waitress came to take his order. "What can I git fer you, honey."

Christian looked up to see the same waitress that always took his order. In three years, she now looked double his age when she was only 2-years older than he. This was the result of a hard life plus she was hitting that stuff or at least so they said.

"Chicken and waffles please," Christian instinctively said. He was not an emotional eater but since he had to deal with Julia, he was going to eat to make himself happy.

"Perfect!" Julia rejoiced at reading Christian's text. She had waited up for him all night long. Steaming a while and being understanding another while. After having a talk with her friend, the wanting to get high on drugs passed over to become replaced by getting high on beating Kenali for Christian's heart.

She strategically planned how she was going to execute her plan. Just when she was about to give up, he replied. No longer having to look out the window to see when he was coming up, she went to dress herself appropriately for the occasion of meeting with Christian— tan, naughty lingerie.

Slipping off her red Maxi dress, which she felt made her look like a sensual goddess, she knew Christian would not be able to resist her. When she put on her lingerie, she twirled in the mirror knowing that her plan was foolproof. The tan color against her complexion made it almost look like she was nude. Skin and stilettos was her first choice. That was just a little too crass even for her.

"One thing my mama always told me is to use what you got to get what you want." Julia smiled assured of herself that Christian would not be able to turn her down. He was going to be so surprised when he sees her. She was going to seduce him so well that he forgot about *old what's her face* and just live happily ever after with her.

Julia decided to run over to the window to see exactly when he was coming in. She was too excited to lie down if it was going to be awhile. To her avail, she had exact timing. Christian was pulling in.

"Showtime," Julia proclaimed grabbing her stilettos putting them on. Then she slid into Christian's bed draping herself seductively with the sheets. She was so excited she was able to coerce a key card out of one of the night hotel workers.

When she heard Christian swipe the card and turn the handle, her heart pumped. The time had finally come. Just as she told her friend only hours before, "I can't lose."

"Good morning, Lane," both Simbol and Kenali sang in unison. They laughed at the thought of sounding like Double Mint twins.

"I'll meet you in the sanctuary." Kenali excused herself to go to the bathroom.

"Ok," Simbol waved a hand at her before turning her attention back to Lane. They went on discussing how the Sunday school class went, how her mom had a hand in his appointment as the teacher, and how much he enjoyed encouraging the kids to take the right path.

Meanwhile, Kenali entered the bathroom placing the flowers on the countertop before going into one of the stalls. When she came out, she saw Ms. Vera sniffing the flowers. Ms. Vera caught a glimpse of Kenali in the mirror, dropped the flowers onto the counter and attempted to run for her dear life.

"Wait, Ms. Vera." Kenali's heart ached at this elderly woman's reaction to her.

Ms. Vera stopped at the door not even turning around. She was stiff as a pole and just about as thin as one also.

"Ms. Vera, I brought these flowers for you."

She only slightly turned her head towards Kenali who was cautiously approaching her.

"For me," her words were quick.

"Yes, ma'am. I wanted to apologize for how I acted the other day at the house. I'm really sorry. I found out that you are Mama's friend."

"Yes, I am," she proudly proclaimed after she turned around to face Kenali. "And I don't blame you for acting like that. A girl's job is to protect they daddy when they mama goes to be with the Lawd. Yo' mama is a good woman."

"Yes, she was."

"No. She *is*," Ms. Vera stressed.

"I don't understand." Kenali almost dismissed it off to Ms. Vera being a little lose in the brain.

"The reason she is because she left a legacy and it is up to you girls, her daughters, to carry it on."

Kenali smiled at the thought. "Thank you, Ms. Vera. I really needed to hear that." Kenali felt a warmness come across her. "Oh. I almost forgot." Kenali extended her arm passing the flowers over to Ms. Vera.

"Thank you, sweetie. These are my favorite kind. How did ya know?" Ms. Vera smiled and sniffed the assorted color mixture of tulips all at the same time.

"I asked one of the dialysis nurses," Kenali humbly smiled. "Now if only I can find out what kind Ms. Beatrice likes."

Ms. Vera's back straightened as well as her face. "Why do you have to buy her some?" Her tone made Kenali feel as if she had gotten jealous that she wasn't the only one.

With caution Kenali answered. "Me and my sister got a little rough with her also until our dad told us that she was Mama's friend also."

Ms. Vera began shaking her head side-to-side. "No. Girl, you remember what I told you about protecting yo' daddy. With that woman, you girls betta get on yo' job. She's a devil and I don't like her!"

Kenali had a lot of concern on her face. Her heart pounded because she didn't know what to do to calm Ms. Vera down. She wondered how much validity was in what she said. "Why do you say that Ms. Vera?"

"Your mama had a rule that she lived by. Keep yo' friends close but keep yo' enemies closer. She been found out about that snake who was full of jealousy." Ms. Vera shook her head, breathing heavily with her mouth tightly balled up. "Baby, it's time for me to give you this now. Yo' mama said that I would know when you girls were ready. It's time."

Kenali watched half of Ms. Vera's arm disappear down into her purse before she came out with three letters. She stared at them as if there was a memory tied to them before she shoved them into Kenali's hand. Then she lovingly patted the back of her hand looking her square in the eye. "I hope to God that she put a warning in there about that devil."

Ms. Vera turned and walked out of the bathroom. Kenali remained looking at the door as it slowly shut behind Ms. Vera. After a moment, she looked at what was in her hand noticing her mother's handwriting on three envelopes. One addressed to each of them; Divine, Simbol and Kenali.

Kenali walked out of the bathroom finding one of the empty classrooms to sit in. She thought about going to get Simbol out of the sanctuary but she felt the press to read her letter now.

"Lord, we did ask for a word when we came to church. I guess this is it."

Kenali took out the envelope addressed to her placing the other two onto the table. Feeling an uncertainty about what she was going to read, she wiped the tears from her eyes before opening it. Pulling the letter out, she slowly unfolded it.

Kenali,

You're my baby girl. I know you might not understand everything that is going on right now but you have to try. First, I know you are probably beating yourself up for not being married or having children but don't. We all make decisions that we wish we could take back a thousand times. Any regret, let it go. Any regret.

Now about my son-in-law, Christian. ☺ Yes he is my son-in-law. I can't explain how I know it will happen but just know that God pressed my heart about it. For the last 3 years, I wasn't worried if you were going to get back together. I just wanted to know when. I wished I would have been there to see but God showed it to me in the spirit realm. He's going to make you happy but that doesn't mean that you won't hurt each other in the process.

Finally, keep a check on your daddy. He and I had a talk about this time not knowing which one of us would go first. We said it was ok for the other to move on with someone else. But men need that extra protection. I guess God always did know that. He sent us three girls. When it comes to another woman, use the woman in you to judge her. If it don't feel right put her to flight. I know you should never tell a child to fight because it's already in them but you put her on the run and get her away from your daddy. If she's nice, accept her even though it's going to be hard for you to do. And just because someone says they're my friend doesn't mean they weren't a foe that I was keeping close by to watch.

I will always love you my baby girl. Please don't grieve so long that you miss the opportunity to live.

Love,

Mama

P.s. Your daddy wasn't saved either when we married but in time he turned out alright. (hint hint).

Tears fell from Kenali's eyes making water stains on the letter. She had received the word that she needed, what Ms. Vera said was cleared up and so much more. She knew that she could place the regret of not making the last lunch with her mom behind her. She knew that her mama wanted her to be happy with Christian even during this time.

Well the opportunity was knocking at her door and she was not going to miss it as her mama stated. She reached in her purse to get her cell phone.

Simbol, can you get a ride back to the house. I got to go take care of something. I have something for you. Give it to you later. Love you sis.

123

Even before she got a reply, she was out the door heading for her car. She knew that she had gotten the word that she needed even though it wasn't the preached word. She would have been so fidgety sitting in church holding this type of information that she wouldn't have heard a word anyone said.

Kenali was making a beeline straight for Christian. She had to ask for his forgiveness and see if they could work on their future of being together. It just felt right in her heart.

"Thanks, Mama."

CHRISTIAN 19

Christian stood outside of Julia's door knocking. He was wondering what was taking her so long to answer the door. On top of that, she wasn't returning his text messages either. *I guess she's giving me a dose of my own medicine*, he thought as he abandoned knocking.

He decide to go to his room to clean himself up. Julia was certain to find him when she was ready. That he was sure of. Besides, she was probably sulking anyway trying to conjure up some sympathy from him. She loved attention; negative or positive. It didn't matter.

He whipped his cell phone back out of his pocket to send Lane a text that they should meet up after he got out of church. He pressed send and walked into his room. Still looking down at his phone, he was startled when he heard a female voice.

"Hey, baby." Julia attempted to lower her voice to make it enticing to him.

"What the—" Christian was beyond perturbed to see her face and even greater when he saw her actions. She was laying in his bed with her legs crossed swinging one of them. This would have been very sexy if it was any other woman but her. Then she had the gall to have on shoes in his bed, which was a pet peeve of his. "How did you get in here?"

Crawling out of bed like a cat, she beckoned with one finger for him to come to her. At first, he thought that she was naked until he realized it was lace the same color of her skin. He didn't even budge. If there was anything that she taught him in their brief dating history it was once you leave her alone, keep it like that. Going back makes it worse. Now that he's been schooled, she didn't stand a chance.

Coming close to him, she pulled on his shirt as if she was attempting to lead his nonresponsive body to the bed. "What's the matter baby? You don't want me."

"Yeah I want you."

Julia was pleased to hear that. Her face lit up.

"I want you to get out my room. That's what I want you to do."

"Christian, how can you say that?" She was offended but she wasn't in the mood to give up. "I've done a lot for you and this is the thanks that I get," her voice was still attempting to be seductive.

"Julia, the only thing you have done is give me a headache. Nobody asked you to come here!" Christian was yelling at the top of his voice. His anger was heightening by the second.

"I came to keep you from making the mistake of letting Kenali misuse you."

She rubbed his shoulder. He swatted her hand away fiercely causing her to flinch away from him.

"A mistake? My only mistake was getting with you. I want you to leave and go back to New York." His words cut her deep.

The drama queen part of her showed up. Tears were coming to her eyes while she grabbed him and repeatedly tried to kiss him. "Don't say that, Christian. I love you and I know we can make us work." She begged him and groped him to the point he had taken all he could take.

"Get off me, Julia." He pushed her away and headed straight for the door. "Be gone when I get back!"

He walked out the door pulling it closed with so much force that the walls of the hallway vibrated. Christian was so mad that he stormed out of the hotel walking past his car. He didn't even know where he was going but all he knew is that Julia better be out of his room when he got back.

After about 30 minutes of walking on the trail through the park, Christian calmed down enough to send Lane a message.

Man call me when you get out of church.
All hell has broken loose. CRAZY woman problems!

"I can't believe Christian is doing me like this," Julia sobbed laying in a fetal position on the floor of Christian's room. He had hurt her feelings so badly that she did not know what to do.

"All I tried to do was love him and keep that witch from misusing him." She reasoned within her own mind what she was doing was admirable.

After a few minutes of tiring herself out crying, she picked herself up looking out the window. She saw his car still outside, so she knew that wherever he was, he was not far. She searched as far as the glass window would allow her too.

Then, as if the cards were in her favor, Kenali pulled up. *Had he called her*, she thought? What man in his right mind would call one woman and tell her that another half-naked woman tried to come onto him in his hotel room where there were no witnesses?

"She's coming to see Christian. I knew I couldn't lose." Julia scurried around looking for her other stiletto that she had thrown across the room when Christian left. Then she ran into the bathroom splashing water onto her face, ruffling her hair and anything else to make it look as if she and Christian had been romping in the sack. "Ok

Christian, since you're too weak to handle this, I guarantee I'll break this up Julia style."

Her confidence level was through the roof. Massive impact is exactly what she was going for. After she got finished with Kenali, there would be no way that she wanted Christian ever again allowing Julia to have him all to herself.

The much awaited knocking on the door interrupted Julia's evil thoughts. She took a deep breath, exhaled and said, "Work it, girl."

She put on the most sexually playful smile that she could come up with. Pulling the door open, "Christian, did you forgot your key?" her voice rang clearly.

When she realized how shocked Kenali looked and that she had saw fully her lingerie, she added an extra layer of injury by pulling back her shoulders to make her breast appear extra perky.

"Oh, I am so sorry. I thought you were my fiancé." Happily placing her hand on her chest to flash a nicely sized solitaire that she had bought for herself as a way of claiming that someone would marry her. She knew the ring would come in handy one day. Today was perfect.

Kenali was so dazed that her speech almost wouldn't come to her. "Fiancé? Umm. Is this Christian *Jackson's* room?" She had to make sure she had the correct Christian.

"Yes, it is. He should be back in a couple of minutes. He just went to get us some ice to cool down if you know what I mean." Julia laid it on so thickly. She was trying to kill not wound.

"Oh. Ok. Thanks." Kenali was very dry. She turned to begin to walk away.

"Who should I tell him dropped by?" Julia knew that she had already won this battle.

Never turning around to face Julia, Kenali sucked her teeth and said, "Don't bother. I'm a ghost of the past."

Watching Kenali disappear down the hallway Julia smirked with the most victoriously evil look in her eye.

"Indeed you are a ghost."

Lane's phone started vibrating in his pocket during service. When looking at the message from Christian, he knew it was serious. With the message mentioning woman problems, he looked over seeing Simbol sitting alone with no signs of Kenali being anywhere.

Aw man, he thought. Lane could not fathom what could have happened between Christian and Kenali that would be such a big problem. His mind turned over multiple times during service. A part of him almost wished service would speed up.

As soon as the benediction came forth, Lane made a beeline for the outside. Then he heard his name. Turning around he noticed that Simbol was hurriedly in pursuit of him.

"Hey. Lane. Whew, you shot out of there so fast I almost couldn't catch you." Simbol tried to catch her breath. "It's not easy trying to run in heels."

"Oh, my bad. Gotta make an urgent call."

"Ok. But is there any way that I can catch a ride. Kenali left me. Said that she had something to do."

"Yeah, I think I know what that something was. It might have a lil something to do with this call I gotta make. Hop in." Lane opened the door for Simbol. She climbed in looking up at him with the utmost concern on her face. She was worried what was going on. She could not wait for him to get into the car.

He opened the door, dialing numbers on the phone. Sitting down in his seat, he placed the phone to his ear but never said anything. Simbol watched his actions waiting for him to say something. She was worried about her sister.

He placed the phone down. "My cuz ain't answering."

"I'm not trying to be in your business but did you say that your urgent call and my sister leaving might be related."

"I just put two and two together."

"What does that mean?"

Simbol needed more information. She could not stand it if something happened to her sister especially during this delicate time.

"I got a text from Christian telling me to holla at him after service cause hell done broke loose and he got woman problems. Kenali wasn't in church. So go figure."

"Oh. I hope that it's nothing. But let me call her." Simbol pulled her phone from her purse. She dialed and got the same result Lane did. "No answer. What are we going to do?"

Lane thought briefly. "Let's swing by the hotel."

Simbol buckled her seatbelt as a sign of agreement. When they reached the hotel, she looked around the parking lot.

"That's the car Christian's driving but I don't see Kenali's."

They both again tried unsuccessfully to reach Kenali and Christian.

"Sit tight, Ms. Sassy, while I go check his room."

"Ok." She submitted.

She continued to look around even scanning the gas station across the street. No sign of her sister anywhere.

Lane disappeared behind the automatic glass doors. Arriving outside of Christian's room door, he noticed that he heard movement. Listening more carefully, he thought that he heard a woman humming.

His knock on the door caused a hush to fall upon the room. He could tell that someone was on the other side watching him. He looked into the peephole. "I know you're looking at me. Why don't you open the door?"

He waited. Then the door parted open just a little ways. A female voice came from behind the door with fear. "Can I help you?"

"I'm looking for Christian."

"Christian isn't here right now."

Lane paused for the voice he heard did not belong to Kenali. "Ummm. When's he coming back? I'm trying to holla at him." Lane tried to look to see if he could see any of this mysterious woman's features but he could not.

"I don't know. He just stepped out for a little while. He didn't say when he was coming back."

"Ok. I'll check back in about 30 minutes."

"Ok." Immediately she closed the door.

Lane walked away with an eerie feeling. Neither Christian nor Kenali were answering the phone. If this mystery lady was up to anything phony his last statement was sure to flush her out of the room. He waited down the hall out of sight.

While he waited, he sent Simbol a text checking on her. She was alright but still no sign of his cousin or her sister. After about ten minutes, his plan started to take action. A woman came flying out Christian's room as fast as her heels would allow her. She looked nervous—very nervous which frightened him with the present situation.

As soon as she got close enough, he walked into her path. He thought that she was going to pass out. The woman behind the shades looked so familiar to him. *Where have we met*, he thought?

"Big L," she shouted with fear.

Big L? This woman knows me from the streets. I haven't been called that in years.

"What's been going on?" He decided to play along with her since she had reason to believe that he recognized her.

She became so nervous that she fumbled her purse until it fell on the floor. *Why was she so nervous?*

"Oh, nothing much. You know me. Just busy, busy, busy. Like now. I gotta go." She then tried to walk past Lane but he caught her by the arm.

"Don't be in such a rush. That's no way to treat an old friend." He was still fishing.

"Look, Big L, I don't do that anymore. I've been clean for five years."

It all flooded him now. He used to refer to her as his Friday Frequent Flyer. Like clockwork she was coming to get her fix on Friday; every Friday sometimes twice. Julia was her name. Lane was the best at face recognition. The business had required it.

And his memory of her was that she was his best customer which is why she was probably so nervous. He tended to get that a lot when he would run across his old customers in stores or restaurants. He always used his exit of that life to calm them.

"Well that's good. I've been out the biz for a while myself. I changed partners if you know what I mean." He flashed a crooked smile. "But I was still trying to get up with my boy."

Collecting this new information, Julia hesitated as if somehow Lane could read her mind to tell if she was lying. Choosing her words wisely, Julia semi-explained.

"Look, we had an argument and he stormed off." For the most part, Julia had told the truth even if there was a tad bit of omission.

Lane thought for a moment rereading Christian's text in his mind. That would explain the hell breaking loose part but was Julia the crazy woman problem as well. He needed more info.

"So y'all must've been together for a minute having lovers' spats like that?" Lane laughed it off as if joking so she would be more willing to divulge information to him.

It worked. Julia's countenance began to change from nervous to normal. "A couple of years," she grinned looking down as if she was a schoolgirl sharing the experience of her first kiss.

A couple of years, he turned over in his mind. "Did y'all meet before he left," Lane was fishing hard.

Her mood was becoming increasingly heightened. *Maybe she like to talk about Christian*, he thought.

"No. We met on the job in NYC."

Bingo! This was the crazy woman that Christian had told him about a while back who was straight up all wrong with her suffocating clutching of a man. It was true what he said about her being attractive. Actually, he could tell that she was clean; her look had greatly been enhanced.

There was one other thing Lane realized Julia did not know—his relation to Christian. Even when Julia was his customer, he knew she was coming from another city, which for secrecy's sake, many of his customers were.

"Oh, ok," he played along. He noticed the ring on her finger pointing it out, "It looks like he'll cool off. He ain't going nowhere with that kind of investment."

Julia squirmed with excitement although she never relayed the fact a marriage to Christian just wasn't going to happen. Silence was her way of agreeing with his comment without having to say it herself.

This chic is real whacked out if she thinks Christian would choose her over Kenali, Lane thought. What he was thinking must have displayed on his face.

"What's that look for?" she asked.

Lane thought fast. "Oh. I remembered I have someone waiting in the ride."

She bought it. Returning to her previous excitement, "Well I don't want to hold you up any longer. It was good seeing you. I'm glad that we both have made changes for the better." Julia was just as perky as if she had just ran into an old competitive classmate that looked a hot mess.

He wondered how long she would live in this fantasy land. He had never seen this type of hallucinations without someone being high. Had he not received the disturbing text from Simbol, he probably would have toyed with her some more.

You cousins are something serious. Tell Christian I never thought he was a player. The last thing my sis needed right now was more hurt. I'm gone. Don't call or text me—ever!!!

By the time Lane reached his ride, he saw his passenger door wide open with no Simbol sitting in it. Had he been in a larger city where he was unknown, his unattended running Escalade would have been long gone just as Simbol was. He didn't understand.

His cousin was right—women are crazy. He did not know which one was worse; the for real crazy one he left upstairs or the stubborn one he had to find out what she was talking about.

"Lord, I got to find a way to get Beatrice away from here before the girls find out the truth. What kind of man would they think I was if they knew what happened?"

Alto sat on the side of the bed with a hung down head. He looked at his slippers that his beloved Pastoria had bought for him. Everything she had gotten for him was always perfect.

"Honey," he hoped his wife could hear him, "you know I didn't mean to do anything against you. You know that right?"

Raising himself from the bed, he went into his bathroom. He couldn't believe that his sweet wife had been gone for seven days already. He certainly was happy that the girls were around the house. It would have been much better had he not had his past mistakes looming over his head.

He exchanged his pajamas for a pair of casual slacks and a button up shirt that he would leave hanging out during his morning walk across his massive backyard that extended far into the forest.

When he opened his door, starting downstairs, he noticed that he was not greeted by the smells of food coming from the kitchen as he had been the last few days.

He charged it off to Simbol probably being up late with Lane.

Lane reminded him of his younger self; running the streets until it was time to give it all up for a better life of peace. Looking at how he turned out minus his one pressing issue, he knew that if Lane and Simbol did get together, as a father he did not have anything to worry about.

There was no sign of Simbol in the kitchen. He opened the refrigerator to get some orange juice. While he drank it, he saw out the window, Kenali sitting under the Magnolia tree out in the backyard. If she was still as she was when she was a child, he knew she had beat every dark green leaf of that tree to ensure there weren't any little critters in it before she got under it. He never seen anything like it; girl raised up around acres of trees and afraid of a frog.

Putting the glass into the sink, he prayed that Christian had not hurt his baby girl, not now of all times. He was fond of Christian but he had not seen him since he left. He never asked why they parted; Kenali never told him. More than likely she talked it over with her mama. Now, he would have to take his wife's place in the emotions department.

"You look like you're having a bad day," he said to his daughter that was pulling up sprigs of grass. "Wanna talk about it?"

Kenali never looked up but only shook her head from side-to-side signifying she did not.

"Well, whenever you want to, I can listen, baby girl" Since Kenali did not make any different movements other than her previous pouting, he began to walk off.

"All men are no good," her words came out strong.

He froze from the comment. Did she somehow find out what he had done all those years ago? Beatrice must have gotten to her somehow. That must be the reason that she could not look at him. He could not hide anymore. He had to explain. "Honey—"

"Dad, Christian is a jerk. I mean I really thought that we actually had a chance," Kenali fumed.

Realizing he almost explained a hurtful past, which would have added more to what she was already going through, caused him to kneel down to hug her tightly. She wept. They were in this same place again one week later both weeping and rocking. She was weeping of another heartbreak; he was for the assessing of the damage he almost caused.

He knew now what he did not know earlier that morning; this problem with Beatrice had to end now before it could gain the opportunity to rob his daughters of any piece of mind. Alto was willing to do whatever it took to protect his family even if that meant finding the right time to tell the truth.

"I got Alto just where I want him," Beatrice turned over last night's phone conversation in her mind. "He's going to regret the day he made Pastoria his wife instead of me."

Beatrice and Pastoria had been friends since they were little. In their lengthy friendship, it always seemed that Pastoria got the better opportunities. Pastoria had the most friends, the longer hair, she was prettier plus the list goes on and on. That was what Beatrice heard ever since they were kids; you should be more like Pastoria. But Beatrice could never fault Pastoria because she never treated her like everyone else did.

Beatrice held onto to the hope of not having to measure up to Pastoria in others' eyes. Then that one day came. Finally, she thought, I got one thing she don't; Alto King, the hottest catch in the city.

Everybody knew he was going to be something. Money was attracted to him and business should have been his middle name. Beatrice already had it planned out after being with him for two weeks. They would get married, have a couple of kids, live in a nice house and be set for life. There was just one hiccup in her plan. Pastoria came home from college stealing his attention, his heart, and his hand in marriage.

At first, Beatrice tried to play it cool pretending that when he stopped calling her it did not hurt. She never even told Pastoria they dated for several reasons. Primarily she was too embarrassed since they were never seen in public together for those short two weeks. Beatrice really could not make the claim of ever being his girlfriend. No one would believe it.

Year after year, she wondered how it would have been if Alto would have married her. On every anniversary that Pastoria and Alto had, Beatrice knew that was supposed to be her getting the jewelry, the vacations, and the cars. Year after year, she toiled in her mind how she could get him even while she was sitting in their living room watching movies with them while she had some second rate boyfriend by her side.

Then one day, five years into Alto and Pastoria's marriage, the perfect set up landed in her lap. Pastoria was out of town at a church convention. Alto came to a house party getting his drink on being the life of the party as usual. All he knew is that he woke up in bed next to Beatrice. She owned the role of making him think that he forced himself onto her. Even though nothing happened, he would never know it.

Therefore, she used that one night long ago, to hold over his head. Alto having one too many that night worked out in Pastoria's and her favor. Pastoria finally got the saved husband she always prayed for. As for Beatrice, financially it had been beneficial to her up until a few years ago.

Beatrice could not believe Alto cut her off like he did. One day she called him for some money and he flat out told her, "No! My kids are way past grown now. And my wife, your supposedly best friend has health problems. So if you want to mess my marriage up over whatever happened back then, that I don't even remember, then go ahead and try! May God have mercy on you if you do?" Then he slammed the phone down.

Although she was merciful back then, talking to Pastoria on a regular hearing her talk about her kidney failure and all the medical costs they incurred, she did not have to be so kind now. She gave Alto an ultimatum last night on the phone.

"Within six months, you either make me your wife or I'll tell your three lovely daughters how you cheated on their mama. Then watch how they turn on you. Understood?"

Beatrice knew Alto was still grieving which meant she had to play this carefully while she still had the upper hand. As she planned to play her cards right, she was going to inflict more damage on that hussy Simbol for calling her a devil. Just by becoming their stepmom would kill those two little birds, Simbol and Kenali, with one stone—2-carat Princess cut. Certainly, Simbol would cease coming around along with Daddy's little girl Kenali. Divine was easier to handle. She was friendly and just as clueless as her mother Pastoria of her intentions towards her father.

Yes. It was going to be a wonderful way to spend the rest of her days. Finally married to the man that was supposed to be hers in the first place spending the money from her poor dead friend's insurance policy. She smiled thinking the saying *good things come to those who wait* could not have been more true.

Kenali sat in the family room sulking. She replayed in her mind repeatedly what happened yesterday. Christian called a couple of times last night but she sent the calls to voicemail. She couldn't believe how much he had changed in three years. Maybe he was trying to pay her back for how she broke up with him. Should that be the case, it was low and cruel with horrible timing.

The phone began vibrating. It was Christian. Very robotically, Kenali tossed the phone over onto the sofa. One thing was for sure, Christian did not have to worry about coming around here anymore. Just as soon as the thought entered her mind, the doorbell rang.

"Christian's outside," Simbol announced with a harsh attitude. Kenali never moved. "Do you want me to throw some hot water out there on him? I betcha he never come around here again."

As tempting the thought were, Kenali felt that ignoring him was going to beat him up worse. Just as he ignored to tell her he was engaged. Several conversations they had would have been perfect to divulge that kind of information. Even the night he stayed, he could have mentioned someone was waiting for him.

Simbol boldly stood with her hands on her hips in clear view to allow Christian to see her through the door.

"He's still out there. He's looking straight at me." Simbol popped her neck at Christian who gestured for her to please let him in. She could hear his muffled voice saying something about wanting to explain.

When she heard the kettle whistling in the kitchen, she grinned devilishly holding up one finger signifying for him to wait one minute. Kenali watched Simbol run past her into the kitchen emptying the contents of the kettle into a boiler. Then she cautiously walked through the house towards the front door being careful not to spill any of the scalding hot water.

Kenali watched until she realized Simbol was serious. She then jumped up from her seat to keep Simbol from accomplishing what she set out to do. When Christian saw the two sisters tussling with the hot water occasionally splashing themselves screaming "ouch" and "let me do it, Kenali", he bucked his eyes realizing that it was time to go.

"See there. Now you let him get away. I could have got him good."

"Simbol, what if dad would have been here? You would have upset him."

"I wouldn't do anything to upset Daddy. But no guy is going to play with my sister. Not now. Not ever!" Simbol was huffing and puffing from the careful tussling with the hot water. "Daddy probably would've knocked him out if he knew the whole story." Walking back into the kitchen with boiler in hand, she poured the water into a coffee cup. "You want a cup of coffee?"

"No thanks." Kenali watched Simbol's prep process from the recliner. "I just can't believe he didn't tell me when he had all the opportunities to do so. Do you think that he was trying to get me back or something?"

"I hope not like that. Especially now. I never figured Christian for the low down type. This is shocking to me."

She sipped the coffee burning her tongue. Holding up her cup, "This definitely would have helped him come back to his normal self."

Kenali began laughing so hard until she felt the need to cry.

"I feel so stupid. Thinking it would work out this time. I should have just went through the grieving process and that's it," Kenali sniffed. "And to think that I asked for a sign."

Simbol thought carefully about the two of them asking for a sign. She giggled.

"Well, the word that you missed was a pretty on time word. The pastor said that our God is the God of a fresh start." Simbol raised her hand into to the air as if she felt the power of the word all over again. "Girl, you should have stayed for that message cause the pastor was on it. He said that just because it didn't work out the last time doesn't mean it won't work this time. Just put your situation on the potter's wheel and let God turn that mess up into a bless up. Hallelujah!"

Listening to Simbol, Kenali wished she had stayed. If she had not gotten the letter from Ms. Vera—.

"I forgot to give you the letter." Kenali sprung to her feet making a mad dash up the stairs.

"What letter?" Simbol asked to an empty swiftly rocking recliner.

Kenali reached her room grabbing her purse digging into it as she ran back down the stairs. Handing it to a puzzled Simbol, "Here," were the only words Kenali spoke.

"What is it?" Simbol cautiously asked rubbing her hand across what she noticed to be her mother's handwriting. She looked up at Kenali with tears forming in her eyes. "Is this from Mama?"

Kenali nodded in agreement. She watched Simbol struggle to open it. Kenali answered Simbol's unspoken question. "Ms. Vera gave them to me this morning."

Those words allowed Simbol to break the seal. Pulling out the letter to begin reading silently, she cried and smiled. "Kenali, this is what I needed. Exactly what I needed. Mama always did know best."

Kenali was happy that her sister got exactly what she wanted but she couldn't resist the feeling that her mama made a mistake in hers. If she knew what Christian was going to do, she would have left his name out the letter. One thing was for sure, Mama did know best about telling her to watch her so-called friend.

Hours later, Kenali and Simbol both watched Divine open her letter. All their first responses were the same; cherishing the fact of their name being written in their mama's handwriting on an envelope. There was something making the reading even more special.

After reading the letter and regrouping, Divine asked, "Did Daddy get one?"

"No. Or at least she didn't give me one." Thinking in silence, Kenali remembered something Ms. Vera said. "She did say that Mama told her to give us these letters when the time is right. So maybe it's not time."

"Yeah, you might be right." Divine paused taking in a deep breath. "What are we going to do about Beatrice?"

Kenali and Simbol looked at each other then back to Divine. Simbol raised her eyebrow and softly yet seriously said, "I know of these people in Georgia that have a money back guarantee."

"A money back guarantee on what?" Kenali questioned.

"If any evidence, a toe or finger, anything is found, you get your money back," Simbol managed to keep a straight face.

"Simbol, are you saying we should kill Beatrice?" Kenali was in shock.

Divine's mouth fell open. "I knew you would say something like that. However, in this case, you are right. We should kill her."

"I know we're grieving but we can't go around killing people," Kenali reasoned.

"Yes we can and we are. Take notes ladies cause this is how we're going to do it."

Divine laid out the plan of action for Simbol and Kenali. She was very detailed in her plan. It was going to be flawless if Kenali could keep her end of the bargain. This was going to be a surefire way to get rid of Beatrice once and for all.

Christian returned cautiously to his hotel room. Thankfully, Julia had left. Closing the door behind him, he latched it so he wouldn't have any more unexpected visitors. Julia had ruined everything for him. Not only did it add unnecessary drama to Kenali's grieving process but it also damaged his newfound hope of getting her back. His coming here was a big mistake.

Had he not put two and two together after running into Lane in the hotel parking lot, he would have never known that Kenali had been here. Simbol's message to Lane said it all—Kenali met Julia. Moreover, if she told Kenali any of the lies that she implied to Lane, then there's no wonder why Simbol would want to harm him.

He fell across the bed allowing his body to lifelessly bounce around until it settled. He wanted most to yell or punch something although it wouldn't help his situation any. Perhaps he could get away with giving Julia a good shaking but that might encourage her in some sick psychotic way.

When it came to Christian shedding his life of Julia, it was so far into craziness that his normal mind did not know how to solve the problem. He thought of Julia as a Lifetime movie full of drama and twisted plots. Figuring from how some of those movies ended, he tried to be careful.

Leaving as he did the first time was the only thing he knew to do. He didn't want to cause more trouble than he had already done. Making up his mind to go back to New York without any further contact felt like tucking his tail and running but it was going to be best for everyone.

Digging in his pocket for his cellphone, the words of the old man at the oasis returned to him. *I can't plant my feet and fight for her if I'm running away,* he thought.

"Why not. What I got to lose?"

His battle plan was becoming clear now. He just realized that his most powerful weapon to getting rid of Julia was Lane.

Christian hopped to his feet, packed his things, and checked out the hotel. He was heading home where it was peaceful and secluded from Julia. Had she known where he was last night, she would have been there. This was going to be the perfect place for him to hide out like a sniper when he fired his first and hopefully most deadly shot.

"Why don't you swing by the hotel and have a little talk with Julia."

Christian filled Lane in on just what to say to get rid of his huge problem. Lane always was very persuasive especially when it came to the ladies. With their history, Julia would definitely not want Christian to know her previous acquaintance with Lane and would make the decision to leave to keep their little secret. His brilliant plan was now in execution.

After Julia was gone and not having to worry about what kind of drama she would cause next, he would find a way to explain everything to Kenali. He loved it when a plan came together especially in his favor.

Thinking back over how things have come together from the advice of a stranger, Christian could do no more than smile.

"Thanks for the advice my old, wise friend."

Julia heard knocking on her door. She beamed just to think that Christian had returned to his senses enough to come apologize to her for how he had treated her.

Choosing to look through the peephole first, she became immediately disappointed.

Oh no! What could he possibly want?

Julia scrambled for what to do while looking at Lane on the other side of the door. Reluctantly opening the door, she greeted him with a fake smile.

"Twice in one day. I take it that you didn't find Christian."

Lane flashed a smile back, "Yeah. I ran into him earlier."

Julia questioned now more than before his reasons for coming to her room.

"Oh? You did?" She became nervous. "So what do I owe this visit to?"

"I need to holla at you for a minute."

About what? Julia's mind screamed.

Noticing that he looked past her as if he wanted an invitation to come in, she complied with the request of his eyes.

"Come on in."

He better not try anything.

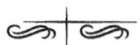

She dismissed the thought when she noticed that he did not have bedroom eyes. She went ahead of him to remove her bag from the couch.

"Have a seat."

"Thanks."

Lane sat on the edge. One thing the streets always taught him was not to get too relaxed in unfamiliar surroundings.

After a weird pause, Julia broke the silence.

"So you said you wanted to talk to me."

"Yes. I do. I need to talk about you and Christian."

"What about?"

Lane sucked his bottom lip thinking of a way to put what he had to say. It was perfect in his head on the way over but now it had dissipated.

"Well, I ain't the one to beat around the bush so I'll come right out with it. Y'all ain't meant for each other."

Julia crossed her arms across her chest. Clearly, she was agitated.

"And why is that? You make it seem like you and Christian talk all the time."

"We do talk a good bit and—"

"Talking a lot doesn't make you a relationship's expert."

"Listening does," Lane shot back. "I listen to Christian say how much he loves someone else. Someone he met long before you."

"She dumped him! How could he still love her?" Julia almost yelled.

"You can't help who you love and if he can't help it, then he just can't help it."

"That's why I came down here. To make sure that she didn't misuse or hurt him anymore than she already has."

"The only one hurting him is you. Look, men don't like drama especially the kind you bringing. You feel me?"

Julia pursed her lips out. She did not appreciate how Lane came to her room to tell her to leave Christian alone.

"All men don't think alike. So just because you don't like—how did you put it—the kind of drama I'm bringing, don't mean that Christian doesn't need me."

Lane sat silently for a moment staring at Julia. He knew that he was going to have to bring out the heavy artillery on her.

"Let me explain something to you. Christian is my boy. We grew up together. We're cousins but we don't tell each other everything especially about the biz I used to be in." Lane paused to lick his lips, which was something that he did when he reached a new level of irritation. He punched his fist into his other hand. "So if you want your skeletons to stay in the closet, then I suggest that you end your little unwelcomed stay in Bama and get up outta here."

Julia stayed quiet momentarily giving Lane the evil stare.

"Get the hell out my room!" she exploded.

Lane walked to the door, looked back at her.

"Remember what I said." He calmly walked out.

Julia kicked the door closed causing it to slam. Her breathing was so heavily out of control. The only thing she could see was fire. She ripped the sheets from the bed, screaming and throwing pillows. One of the pillows knocked the lamp over but she didn't care. She then lay on the bare mattress sobbing in defeat not knowing what to do.

Her mind was swarming with confusion. If she left as Lane had suggested then she would lose Christian forever but if she stayed she would be exposed to him as an exjunky. With either one of those options, she would wind up losing.

"I need something to settle me down so I can think."

No longer fighting the urge, she combed the streets looking for someone in the biz that Lane had given up. After getting what she needed, she now knew what she was going to do—make Kenali's life a living hell.

"Look, Kenali, you're my sister in Christ and I wouldn't tell you nothing wrong. You gotta give my cuz another chance. He didn't do anything wrong. I'm serious," Lane pleaded.

Kenali was very stern. She was holding her guard up and Lane did not blame her.

"All I know is that this *naked* woman in *his room* said that she was engaged to Christian," Kenali looked at him forcing him to explain that.

"He's not. They dated a while back in NYC. He broke up with her but she ain't accepting that."

"Christian ain't all that," Simbol blurted out. "My bad. Go ahead."

"Why would she be here if they broke up?" Kenali demanded.

"Cause she ain't right in the head."

"She was in his room."

"She stole a key."

"Yeah. Whatever."

None of this made any sense to Kenali. This was supposed to happen in works of fiction not in her life.

"I'll have to think about this but now is not the time. I already got too much on my plate."

"I understand that." Lane let it go. "So how you holding up?"

"Taking it one day at a time. That's all I can do."

"I'm still praying with y'all that peace comes."

"Thanks, Lane. We need all the prayers we can get. Just miss Mom so much."

"Yeah. I miss her too," he paused. "You know she wouldn't let nobody judge me. Mrs. King helped me out a lot that first year I got saved. If it wasn't for her, I would be back on the streets slanging dope. She'll always be my angel."

Simbol tuned in extra sympathetically to Lane while he expressed his gratitude for her mama. What was written in the letter from her mama all made sense now. Her mama had endorsed Lane because she knew that he was saved for real and the right man to make her most stone hearted daughter happy.

"That's sweet, Lane," Simbol said before pausing. "And thank you for coming over to calm things with Christian and my sis. It's good to know Christian wasn't being a jerk."

She still did not say the one thing that she originally was going to say.

I hate apologizing.

Exhaling heavily, "Oh yeah. I'm sorry about the other day. I didn't mean what I text you."

Lane flashed one of those handsomely crooked smiles.

"No need to apologize. I would have done the same if the tables were turned."

He dug into his pocket retrieving his phone to begin texting.

Simbol and Kenali looked at him wondering what on that phone was so important.

"Well that's just rude. You stopped talking to check your phone," Simbol scolded.

156

Then her phone began beeping. She read it smiling.

I accept your apology. Can I call you tonight?

Lane crossed his fingers while he watched her read it. He was so adorable in his own way, Simbol thought while sending him a reply.

Too grown for all this texting. LOL. Looking forward to it. ;-)

Lane could not believe that he was acting like this with his grown self. It was something about Simbol that just brought out the playful side of him; the side that was never allowed to come out because of his past.

Mrs. King was right when she told him that when he met the right woman, she was going to make him feel different on the inside. Simbol was the manifestation of her mama's words.

"Alto sure is mighty bold telling me to leave his family alone. I can't believe that he turned down my proposal that we get married or I tell his kids. He must think that I'm joking. I'll show him that I mean business."

Beatrice was so livid that she talked aloud to herself. The only thing that busted this solo conversation up was seeing Alto's home number pop up on her cell's caller id.

"Have you had a change of heart?" she asked hoping that he would say yes.

"Excuse me?" a female voice questioned. "Is this Beatrice?"

Beatrice gasped from her blunder.

"Oh, yes. It is."

"This is Simbol and I really wanted to call you to apologize for how I acted the other day. This is a hard time for me right now."

Wow. Beatrice could not believe that she had Simbol on the phone apologizing.

"Honey, I understand. I accept."

"Thank you. Dad told us how long you and Mama were friends and that's no way to treat you."

Beatrice winced at the phrase of being friends.

❧ | ❧

"Yes. Even since we were children." Beatrice rolled her eyes before continuing. "I sure do miss Pastoria," she lied.

"Yes. We do too. And since you two were such good friends we wanted to get to know you better."

Beatrice was thinking this was going to work out better than she thought.

"So my sisters and I would like to invite you over tomorrow for lunch so we can have a chat."

Beatrice smiled at the opportunity to get closer to the girls so that it would make her blow even harsher than previously planned.

"Honey, I would love that. What time should I arrive?"

"Is noon fine with you?" Simbol so politely chimed.

"Certainly. I'll see you then."

Beatrice talked on a whole new level. Her plan was working. Just because Alto closed one door did not mean that another door would not open. And to think that his very own daughters opened it made this game even sweeter.

"She bought it!"

Simbol looked into the eager faces of Kenali and Divine. She smirked at the thought of having the upper hand.

"We can finally put this heifer down like she's supposed to be," Divine added.

Kenali smiled and nodded. All three sisters knew what part they would have to play tomorrow for getting rid of this devil.

As soon as darkness fell, Julia was prepared to unleash phase one of hell on earth for Kenali. She was feeling pretty empowered especially since she was high as a kite.

Dressed in all black from head to toe, Julia intentionally parked a great distance from Kenali's house. Pulling her hoodie over her head grabbing her bag of goodies from the front seat, she began a slow jog until she could see the red door that marked Kenali's house.

Her mind marveled over the white, black, and yellow spray paint she'd gotten that was going to turn the door and entire house into a new work of art. She thought of what she would title her masterpiece but chose to wait until she was finished to see what name her work inspired.

Speed racing up the walkway, she grabbed a can of spray paint. Spraying the words that Kenali deserved to be called, she covered the entire door running out of room therefore using the brick as extra canvas space.

Occasionally, she would look around to see if anyone was watching her. Remembering that the nearest neighbor was about 100 yards away, Julia then would look back towards her masterpiece smiling wondering what else to do. She whistled while she worked.

After all three cans of paint had been used all around the entire house, she then grabbed the lead pipe from her bag. When she broke the first window, the alarm went off

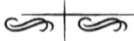

spoiling her fun. Taking off to run, she decided to break another window since she had to pass by it anyway.

Christian will regret the day he sent his dog to my room to do his dirty work.

She has never been the one to appreciate being told what to do or where to go. Full of determination, she was going to show them what they had unleashed.

Breathing heavily as she got into her car to speed away, she began to laugh uncontrollably. Her plan was going to work. She rejoiced at how clearly she was thinking just after taking one hit.

Next, she figured she should go pay Christian a little visit at the hotel since she still had the key. Even though when she pulled into the parking lot she did not spot his car, she decided to go in to leave him a little message anyway.

Julia used one of the side entrances keeping her hoodie on with her head down, she ran up the stairs. She did not want to be spotted since she had already checked out the hotel and used another ID to book somewhere else. She was always resourceful and it paid off once dating a guy that had a job making driver's licenses.

Swiping the key in the door, the red light flashed. She could not figure out what was wrong. She tried it again getting the same result. Then she realized that Christian had probably checked out already.

He could be staying with Big L.

Dismissing the idea of finding where Lane lived, she recaptured her last act of devilment grading her work by looking at the photos that she had taken on her cell. Just then, the most perfect title came to her. *When a Woman Loves a Man.* There had been so much passion put into what she was doing and all of it was fueled by the love she had for Christian.

"That'll teach you to reject me, Christian Jackson."

"My alarm is going off?" Kenali repeated what she heard. "Thank you for sending the police out. I'll go right over."

Kenali looked at the phone after she hung up.

Simbol and Divine watched her with such intensity as they only heard her part of the conversation.

"What's going on?" Divine questioned.

"The alarm company said that my alarm had been triggered. It's probably nothing like the last time this happened. I'm going to go over to check it out."

"Alone? No you're not." Divine interjected.

"The police is on the way. I'm going to meet them there."

"Either me or Divine is going with you regardless of what you say."

"Amen, sistah," Divine cosigned.

Knowing that she was not going to win this concerned double team, Kenali did not argue.

"Whichever one of you it is, meet me at the car," she said as she hurriedly walked towards the front door grabbing up keys and her purse.

Divine and Simbol looked at each. Then Simbol started a pursuit behind Kenali.

"I can fight better than you can."

"Whatever. I'm the oldest."

"My point exactly."

Simbol flashed a large smile exposing most of her teeth as she closed the door behind her.

Kenali drove the familiar route from her parents' home to hers. It was only a 15-minute ride.

"What if it's not a ghost alarm, what are you going to do?"

Kenali thought about what Simbol asked, pressing the accelerator harder turning the trip into 10-minutes instead.

Even from a distance, she could see the police lights flashing. With them walking around the house, she knew that it was not a false alarm.

She read the profanities that had been spray painted all over her house as she pulled into her driveway. Her mouth was wide open in disbelief.

"What in the world," Simbol started.

Kenali with Simbol in tow, walked towards one of the officers. He recognized her.

"Ms. King, I'm sorry that this had to happen especially at a time like this. We've assessed the damage and don't think that they made it into the house. We have been having a string of vandalisms lately in which we're trying to catch the perpetrators which are probably some teens that need their backside heated up."

"Some teens?" Kenali repeated still in shock.

She looked over at Simbol with a question in her mind. They both knew the particular teen that did this was in her thirties yet she still needed her backside heated up for acting liked a brat.

"Yes ma'am. Could you go into the house to see if anything has been taken?"

Kenali looked at her ring of keys finding her house key. She unlocked the door and instinctively shut the alarm off. Kenali walked around with Simbol and the police officer.

"Everything in here is still as I left it."

"Ok. Maybe the alarm spooked them. We are going to do everything that we can to find out who did this. Were you going to stay here tonight?"

"No. I've been staying with my dad since the funeral." Kenali was just numbly answering questions.

"Once again, Ms. King, we're sorry that this has happened to you especially now."

"Thank you. I appreciate it."

"Well, we're going to be outside finishing up our report and taking photos. If you can think of anything or you need something, just let us know."

"I certainly will," Kenali said following the officer to the door.

Looking back at Simbol, Kenali was thinking. Most likely they were the same thoughts that Simbol was having.

"Man stealer? Why would a teen write that? You know the person that wrote that is most likely that nut that's following Christian."

Simbol was a new level of upset that she referred to as 38 hot.

"This is all so stupid and confusing to me. Why would she come do something like this when I've done nothing wrong to her?"

"Because that chic is crazy. Normal people won't get what's going through her head to make her do what she does," Simbol had a flashback. "They just make your blood boil especially when they play innocent. Ugggh! Just makes me wanna choke somebody."

Simbol had dealt with Julia's kind before. She couldn't stand when adults played childish games and then walk around fronting to be grown.

Kenali looked at the anger that had consumed Simbol wondering why she could not get equally as angry. After all, it was her house, her emotions, and her heart that had been broken. Perhaps the newness of the experience had disabled her.

Simbol was still pacing back and forth, trying to think of what to do.

"Tell the police you know who did it," Simbol blurted out.

"But I don't know who did it."

"Yes, you do! You know it was her."

"I can't prove it. I can't just go tell the police that some lady lied about being engaged to a man I broke up with. Then a couple of days later she vandalized my house. That makes it look like I'm trying to get back at her."

Momentarily thinking about it, Simbol had to agree.

"Yeah. You got a point. I just wished that I knew who could help."

The timing could not have been more perfect for her cell to start ringing. It was Lane calling as he promised but he just didn't know that he was the answer to her prayer.

"Just the person I needed to talk to," Simbol answered.

"Oh, yeah. Sounds like music to my ears," Lane was pleased.

"Well, what I have to tell you isn't going to be very melodious."

Simbol filled Lane in on everything that was going on over to Kenali's. He was upset in his calm collected way. He must have been riding while he was talking to her. No sooner than she hung up the phone, he and Christian were coming through the door.

Simbol was concerned about her sister since she still had an eerie silent thing going on. Simbol credited it to Kenali still being upset about the hotel visit.

The look on Christian's face was apologetic and as badly as Simbol wanted to get him, she could not fault him for things out of his control. She hoped that Christian's presence would help Kenali in some way.

Kenali looked at Christian with eyes that could have cut glass. He approached her against his better judgment. After being silent the entire time, she was now ready to speak.

"Stay away from me!" she yelled.

Her words captured the attention of Lane and Simbol. Christian was so shocked. He was wounded and embarrassed.

"Ever since you've been here, it's been one thing after another. The best thing to do is just leave me alone!"

Tears erupted from her eyes as she ran down the hallway to her bedroom forcefully slamming the door behind her. Kenali did not mean to yell at him but somebody had to pay for her mother dying, having to deal with Beatrice, having her feelings stomped in the mud at the hotel and now this destruction of her home. Since Christian was linked to about two of them, he was the best target for her.

Simbol knocked at her bedroom door. There was no answer.

"Kenali," she cautiously called as she carefully entered the room.

Kenali was on the bed heaving. From the look on her face, the ranting was nowhere near being over.

"I'm stressed, Simbol! Yet everybody expects me to keep it together. All these things are being dumped in my lap back-to-back and I can't take anymore!"

Kenali was shaking uncontrollably. Simbol greatly sympathized with her. She wrapped her arms around her baby sister rocking and crying with her.

Christian heard her words. He knew that it was a mistake to come here. He should have followed his own mind; come to the funeral, show support, and leave. Had he left, Kenali would not be going through all of this. His attempt to plant his feet had backfired on him. He was deeply regretful to the point that he was pissed.

"Take me to my car," he ordered Lane as he headed to the door.

"You think it's a good idea to leave now?"

"Leaving is the best thing that I can do for her."

"I don't think you should go see that chic. It only seems to get worse," Lane reasoned.

Christian's mind was set. There was not going to be anymore avoiding Julia. He was tired of playing games. Enough hurt and damage had been done that Julia was going to get her share of it tonight.

"Since you're not changing your mind, I'll swing you by there. That way I can talk you out of killing her."

"Cool," was Christian's only reply.

He was silent, dwelling mentally on what he would say to her; how he could convince her to see on this side of sanity without trying to strangle the life out of Julia. Her actions had proved that she was heartless. Nobody would do something like this to someone grieving. At least no one in his or her right mind.

Even before Lane could stop his truck, Christian had jumped out, walking hard and furiously into the lobby. The clerk behind the desk thought about calling the police in advance. The look on Christian's face said that he was about to murder someone.

Getting onto the elevator, he faced the doors with his shoulders squared significantly more than usual. The vein in the side of his neck had surfaced and was pulsing. Looking at his angry reflection on the stainless steel doors, he concluded that he didn't even want to mess with himself.

The elevator finally dumped him out onto the floor that Julia was staying. He pounded at her door. He heard a small voice on the other side causing him to become even more enraged.

Why is she trying to disguise her voice? Such an idiot.

His thoughts were just as harsh as he was going to be with her if she opened the door. He wasn't the type to beat a woman but Julia was going to get a good shaking tonight.

"Julia, you have 3 seconds to open this door or I'm kicking it down!"

He waited. The door cracked open with the first thing he noticed was a shaking, wrinkly hand with a matching face peeping around.

"I don't know Julia. I just checked in and don't want no trouble."

Tears were almost in this elderly lady's eyes. Her snow white hair as stiff as it were, was even trembling.

Christian calmed himself enough to apologize. However, he was still on a mission to find that crazy woman Julia before she did anything else. He opted for taking the stairs counting on that being the faster route. When he reached the lobby he went straight to the clerk.

"Look man, I don't want no trouble," the male clerk said sizing Christian up by his angered countenance.

"Julia Vile, room 606, when did she check out?"

The clerk typed in the computer as fast as he could.

"She checked out Sunday, yesterday at 7:39p.m."

Christian calculated the time in his head. That was after she had caused her big bang of confusion by breaking into his room. The information appeased him to the point that he walked off without saying a word. The clerk was relieved. Then Christian spun on his heels to come back. Thinking how tricky Julia was.

"Did she check into another room?"

The clerk checked almost wishing that she had not. He did not want to be the one responsible for her death. He shook his head thankfully side-to-side.

When Christian walked through the glass doors, the clerk leaned over the desk to make sure he was gone before he pumped his chest out as if he was never afraid.

"Let me guess? She ain't there."

"Nope."

"Where do you think she disappeared to?"

"She probably went to another hotel. I'll check them all until I find her," Christian vowed.

"She's a ghost in this city. I had someone check them all. That chic ain't in none of 'em."

Christian thought for a moment about her whereabouts. He pulled his cell out of his pocket to start dialing a number that was just downright loathsome to him.

Julia answered the phone in the sweetest voice as if she had done no wrong.

"Hey, honey. Have you stopped being mad at me?"

Christian's teeth chattered at the sound of her voice wishing he could reach through the phone. He clenched his teeth together hard to prevent saying what he wanted to say in the harsh tone that he felt like saying it.

"Where are you?"

"I like how you ignored my question," Julia giggled. "However, I'm in Atlanta. I am on vacation and didn't want to waste my last few days being bored and stuck in that hotel."

He had the feeling that she was lying but how could he prove it.

"How long have you been there?"

"Ever since last night. You should come join me. It'll only take you three hours to get here."

"No thanks. Have you thought about going to the airport to go home?" *Three hours' drive is too close for comfort.*

"Look, I know that you're trying to get rid of me. Coming to Alabama, for me, was a big mistake but I learned a lot. You made the message loud and clear that you don't want me. So, I'm going to enjoy the rest of my vacation and see you back at work next week. Just as easy as that. I'm a big girl. I'll get over you. Besides there are some hot and ready men here that will make a suitable replacement for you. I've always been a sucker for a Down South Stallion."

Christian felt a huge relief come over him. She apparently wanted to evoke jealousy within him but it was not going to happen after all the hell she had put him through. He could not believe it was over.

"Ok. See you at work."

He hung up the phone even before she could give her salutation. He had enough of her for a lifetime. When the time came, he would deal with her at work but for now, he just wanted to go home to chill to get his mind off these events.

"Hey man, my cribs to the left," he vocalized as Lane turned the wrong way.

"Yeah. I know. The streets taught me that if someone is making too many turns behind you, don't go home."

Christian looked into the side mirror noticing the headlights of a car lingering way behind.

"How long have they been behind us?"

"Since the hotel."

"I wonder if it's…"

Christian did not want to say her name. In part, he thought she was lying about being in Atlanta but part of him desperately wanted to believe that she had moved on.

"Only one way to find out."

He made turn after turn with the mystery car in tow until he turned into the house where he used to sell from.

Lane thought he noticed a hesitation of the car but they soon passed by. The darkness plus having tinted windows prevented them from seeing into the car. However, it was not the car that Julia was driving the last time that they saw her. Maybe it was just their minds playing tricks on them with all this madness going on.

Christian felt much better once he reached the one place he knew he could always call home. He wished that place could have been in Kenali's heart. He accepted the fact the road had ended for him and Kenali. There was one sane thing that Julia said that he was going to have to apply to his own life; coming here for me was a big mistake but I learned a lot.

Christian jumped up from a nightmare with his heart pounding hard in his chest. In his dream, there was nothing but darkness surrounding him but he could feel something pulling on him. He could hear Kenali's voice faintly calling out desperately to him although whenever he answered she never heard him. Then whatever was pulling on him started to painfully claw him. Without warning he began to fall very fast causing a sick feeling in his stomach. He fell so far that he could no longer hear Kenali's voice but instead it was replaced with something more terrifying.

Julia repeatedly screaming, "You're mine forever!"

Now fully awake, he knew what to do. His mom had raised him in the church. Although he didn't do everything right, he knew when to pray. Kneeling down in the same spot that she had every night for years, he made an attempt to do what he had not done in so long.

God's not going to hear me.

He countered his own thought to try it anyway in simplicity.

"Lord, help me."

"**I** can't believe they invited Beatrice here for lunch. I don't want that scandalous woman in my house. I'm just going to make it through today and then let her know that she's not welcomed here—ever!"

Mr. King regretted the day he told his daughters to be nicer to Beatrice. He figured if they kept mistreating her that she would expose him. Never did he like the feeling of someone holding something over his head especially something on the magnitude of what Beatrice had on him.

He could not believe he actually slept with that woman. Time after time, he kept trying to think back but nothing would ever come in that area. He always guessed that he blocked it out from pure shame. Pastoria was a really good wife to him and he may have flirted with a few women at parties but never sleeping with them.

Regret came heavily upon his heart.

I could lose my girls' respect.

He thought about how Kenali had turned on poor Christian. He imagined they were in similar situations, not understanding what was going on with women flying off the handle, setting him up and lying on him. He wanted to talk to Kenali about the situation with Christian but he was afraid that if it comes down to her finding out the truth of what he had done years ago, she would call him a hypocrite.

Not needing to lose anything or anyone fueled his desire of wanting to get out of there more than ever. He headed downstairs to see if maybe he could slip away unnoticed. Knowing that he could always use the excuse of the lunch evading his mind, but it would only be effective if no one was downstairs.

Darn, just my luck.

Divine walked through the front door.

"Hey, Daddy."

"Hey there. Let me give you a hand."

He really wanted to give her a hand across her backside for setting up this lunch but instead he helped her with the groceries that she was carrying.

"Daddy, thanks for letting us have Ms. Beatrice over. We really did want to show her and you that we are not as mean as it seems."

This is the one time that you need to be mean as a junkyard dog.

"Oh. You're welcome, honey."

"What are you going to do until lunch?"

"I'm going to just wander around."

Wandering off would be better.

"Ok. Everything will be ready to go in about an hour. Simbol and Kenali will be back soon."

At the mentioning of Kenali, he thought about the events that happened last night over at her place.

"Did they find out who those bad tail kids were?"

"No. Not yet."

Shaking his head in disgust, "I'll call my buddy down at the sheriff's office tomorrow to see what's going on."

Mr. King walked out the back door to piddle around the yard until that dreadful time came when he had to sit at the same table with Beatrice. He hadn't heard from her since he declined her marriage proposal. He couldn't believe that she tried to make him marry her. And even her reasoning was crazy.

"Cause you met me first," she had pathetically said.

He could not believe that women acted like this. The way that some of them carried on made him super glad to be a man. For men—well except for Christian of course—life was simpler.

After the appropriate time had passed, he decided to walk back closer to the house. The closer he got, the more he could see Beatrice sitting in his house that he shared with his wonderful wife. The more he thought of what she was trying to do, the more that he wished he wasn't a church going man. He was a great shot with a gun. Even at his age now, he would have shot through that window knocking her over. He would have gotten away with it too; shooting at something else and missed, is what he would tell them. Case closed. Problem solved.

When he entered the door, her voice was the first to ring out.

"Hey, Alto," she sounded so giddy.

She could have won an Oscar for the female version of Dr. Jekyll and Mr. Hyde.

He almost just threw his hand up going about his business as usual but he saw that squint in her eye.

"Hey, Beatrice. How are you doing?"

"I'm doing well," she answered back. Changing her voice to be more sympathetic, "how are you holding up?"

The gun idea was becoming better and better. She didn't care not one bit about anything or anybody other than herself especially Pastoria.

"Just taking it one day at a time."

"Well I am sure glad that you invited me over for lunch."

"Trust me. It wasn't my idea. It was all the girls' fault—I mean doing," he paused. "Please excuse me for a minute."

He walked away going into the guest bath. He had to talk to himself in the mirror after realizing he was being a bit dry and lose at the mouth for someone who had a secret to hide.

"Behave before she makes you pay."

After rejoining everyone else, he inquired what time the devastation was going to begin so he can estimate how long he would have to endure.

"What time are we going to eat?"

"We're waiting for one more guest," Divine sang from the kitchen.

Oh, great! Another person to watch me be on pins and needles.

"Who is it?"

"A *real* good friend of Mama's that we're apologizing to," Kenali stressed.

"Since I'm the only man in the room just call me when she gets here. I'm feeling a little beat and I want to go upstairs to lie down for a moment."

He could not stand the idea of having to be in the same room for another moment with Beatrice. Maybe they would just forget to call him at all giving him an escape. One thing is for sure, when he got up those stairs, he was going to have another talk with Jesus and hope the Lord heard his cry—I can't lose my girls too.

This is so perfect, I couldn't have planned it better across all those years that I waited. He's lost his prized Pastoria. The last thing he wants to lose now is his darling daughters. I could see it in his face.

Beatrice was so caught up into her thoughts she did not hear Divine talking to her.

"Oh!" she jumped, "I didn't hear you."

"I just asked if you wanted anything else to drink."

Being waited on hand and foot by Pastoria's daughters was a pleasure all of its own.

"Of course, sweetie. Thank you so much."

"Would you like to try some of these cheese straws? They are my favorite."

"Thank you, Simbol. I just love cheese."

Beatrice would have never thought in a million years that she would have went from being a devil to being offered Simbol's favorite snack. She was eating all the attention up so much that she almost felt sorry for what she was going to do. But a girl's gotta do what a girl's gotta do. And now she had to go put some heat under Alto.

"Excuse me for a moment. I have to go to the little girl's room," she giggled.

When she reached it, she looked back seeing that they could not see her from where they were sitting. She scurried up the stairs.

She cracked Alto's door looking in noticing that he was on the side of the bed on his knees.

"That's a good position for you to propose to me from."

She was careful not to raise her voice too much. Nevertheless, she still startled him.

Coming all the way into the room, shutting the door behind her, she continued.

"It doesn't matter if we go to the courthouse or have a great big fabulous wedding. I'll leave that minor detail up to you."

"Look, Beatrice I'm not going to marry you. You might as well leave now."

He stood up turning around hovering over her.

She took note of his body language.

"Alto, are you threatening me?" she grinned pursing her lips out. "How about I just go downstairs and tell those lovely, kind daughters of yours what you did? Come on, let's go."

She turned to reach for the door. He grabbed her hand on the knob.

"Beatrice, why are you doing this now? I just lost the love of my life."

Not even turning around, she clapped slow and dramatically.

"Bravo. The way I recall it is that you weren't that sympathetic to me. You just left me the minute you laid eyes on Pastoria. No warning. No nothing."

"I didn't know you were friends," he defended.

She swung herself around.

"Yeah right! Nevertheless, you are going to pay. The way I figure it, the insurance should be cutting you a check

179

soon and as your wife, I'll have the right to all of it. We'll call it back pay for cutting me off years ago."

"That's what this is all about—money? I'll write you a check right now to get rid of you."

"No, honey. I'm going to spend the money, I'm going to stay in this big fine house, drive the fancy cars in the garage and collect the check whenever you decide to die. All this would have been mine anyway."

Beatrice straightened her clothing, nodded her head, and walked out the door leaving Alto standing there dumbfounded.

She tiptoed around the corner, leaning slightly over the rail to peek to see if the downstairs occupants could see her. Making her way down the stairs in a haste, she went back to her previous seat as if she didn't just have an argument with Alto. According to their actions, they suspected nothing, which was just the way she liked it. Before they knew it, she would move in and be their stepmom right under their pretty little noses.

"**I**f I have to serve that heifer one more thing, I'm going to lose it. What's taking her so long to get here?" Simbol questioned trying to keep her voice low.

"I don't know. She said she was almost here," Divine reassured.

"That was 30-minutes ago," Kenali added.

At the sight of Beatrice coming around the corner, Divine hushed her sisters.

"Was everything alright for you, Ms. Beatrice?"

"Yes, darling it was."

"You want so more cheese straws?" Simbol asked so flatly that Kenali had to kick a smile onto her face. Simbol smiled through the pain of a shin that was definitely going to display a bruise.

Hearing the doorbell ring gave Simbol a real reason to smile. She almost skipped to the door.

"I'm so glad that you are here. *Really*. Come on in."

Simbol led their guest into the family room where everyone else was sitting. She noticed a strange twitch crawl across Beatrice's face.

"Ms. Beatrice, this is Ms. Vera. One of Mama's real, real good friends," Simbol announced with great joy. "Ms. Beatrice, did I offer you some more cheese straws?"

Beatrice fumbled over her words. "Hey, umm, Vera. I haven't seen you in ages."

Ms. Vera stared at her intensely before answering never cracking so much as a smile.

"Yes, it has been a long time."

Simbol looked back and forth between the both of them.

"You two know each other? This is such a small world." Turning her attention to her sisters, "Divine and Kenali, they know each other," she announced in a childlike manner.

"This is going to be an interesting lunch where we can talk about the old times that you both shared with Mama," Divine chimed in.

"I'll go get Daddy," Kenali said before ascending the stairs.

When their daddy reluctantly came down to join the rest of them, he tried to excuse his way out of their company by using the reasons that it was all ladies and he was tired. But the girls just wasn't having it. They insisted he stay. Divine, Simbol and Kenali were on their Ps and Qs with serving up such a good meal.

Ms. Vera still hadn't smiled not a wink. Her lips were tight and her face was unmovable as cement. Their daddy still looked drained. And Beatrice couldn't be read; either she was nervous or excited.

"This table is too quiet," Simbol said in hopes of getting a conversation started.

Still no one said anything. Divine decided to give it a try.

"So, Ms. Beatrice, tell us your earliest memory you have of Mama."

Beatrice readjusted herself in her seat.

"Well, we knew each other since we were kids, it's hard to just pick one."

Simbol not liking the answer added, "Just let it rip. Let *alllll* of the past out. That's the only way that we can know things."

Her daddy flinched. *Simbol is going to start something ugly in here if she keeps it up.*

"She's right." Divine included. "We are just trying to connect the dots. Because you and Mama knew each other since you were kids but we've never really heard anything about you until now. Why is that?"

Beatrice squirmed in her seat rubbing her hands up and down on her thighs, which had to be a sign of nervousness. She looked into every face seated around the table with all of them looking back except Alto.

"Well, I don't know," she hesitated. "That's something that you have to ask your father."

Their daddy kept looking into his plate.

"But, Ms. Beatrice, actually you're the one that has known Mama the longest, even longer than Daddy and I can't ever recall her mentioning your name," Kenali questioned.

Still rubbing her thighs now more violently than before, she had to have known something was up.

"I don't know. We talked on the phone quite a bit every month."

"Yeah so we heard. But still I'm the oldest and Mama never mentioned you to me. I think that's quite strange. So why don't you tell us why that is?"

Divine was very firm in her speaking nearly demanding Beatrice to come clean.

Feeling trapped, Beatrice did the only thing that she could think of.

"Your father has an announcement," Beatrice blurted out.

Almost choking on his food, he looked up with widened eyes. "No I don't!"

Speaking through clinched teeth, "Yes, you do! Either you tell them or I tell them. You remember what we talked about."

He looked cornered and helpless. He knew that the truth was going to set him free. He could only pray that his daughter's would forgive him. It was time to free himself of this heavy load.

"Beatrice is trying to force me to marry her."

Every mouth at the table flew open including the once stone-faced Ms. Vera.

"Force? Alto, tell it right or I'll tell it. Your daddy is such a kidder," Beatrice attempted to laugh it off.

"Yes! Force me. A long time ago, I made a mistake. I had been drinking and she and I—girls, please forgive me. I can't lose you. But she and I—"

"Nothing happened!" Ms. Vera jumped in. "I was there that night. You were out cold. She struggled to get you to her bedroom and she wore herself out trying to get you undressed."

He looked so relieved that if it weren't for his age, he probably would have done a somersault.

"Nothing happened?"

"You're telling a lie! He forced himself on me!"

Beatrice tried to sound convincing. She stood up as if she was going to leave the table.

"No, he didn't heifer!" Ms. Vera walked strong behind Beatrice. "I told Pastoria what you had done. Some kind of friend you are. That hurt her very much. She got a letter for you too."

"Oh, yeah? Then give it here," Beatrice demanded. "Maybe it will clear up some of this mess that I don't have to take."

"I ain't giving it to yo' lying tail." Looking towards Divine, "You're the oldest. You read it."

Ms. Vera pulled the letter from her purse and handed it to Divine. Divine hurriedly opened the letter. Ripping the trifold sheet of paper out, allowing the envelope to fall to the floor. She cleared her throat before she began reading.

Beatrice,

If this letter is being read then that means the devil in you was trying to trap my husband by something you made him think happened in the past. I knew the consequences of dating an unsaved man but I loved him and was determined to pray him through. I never thought that I had to pray him away from the evil vices of someone that was supposed to be my best friend. The reason that I kept you close all of those years was so I could keep a watch on you. God has a way of warning His people who is for or against us. And you've coveted my marriage for so long. A man is going to do what a man is going to do but a friend is supposed to stick closer than a brother or sister. Not in our case.

But here's the dagger that's going to kill the witch in you. Alto is saved and filled with the Holy Spirit. He is forgiven for the past by God Almighty and me. He's free and I pray he remembers it.

-Pastoria

P.S. Get away from my family! Leaving on your own would be better than if my girls helped you to. They can be something serious. They're fierce like their mama.

As soon as Divine finished reading the letter, she looked up at Beatrice almost daring her to say one mumbling word. Beatrice was speaking gibberish. All the eyes in the room were on her. She was definitely outnumbered.

"There must be some kind of mistake," nervously talking and laughing. "I don't know what Pastoria was talking about. Ok. I think I'll just go."

Simbol had already walked to the door to open it. Kenali stood with her arms crossed. Divine had her hands on her hips.

Beatrice remembered the letter stating leaving on her own would be better. She walked backwards as to keep an eye on each of them. She grabbed her purse as she went. When she got to Simbol at the door, it was like déjà vu.

"I hate cheese straws! I got them for the rat in you."

Simbol didn't blink. Then just from impulse, she threw the bag of cheese straws at Beatrice.

"Get to stepping, Boo!"

Kenali gave Simbol instructions.

"Simbol, do your thing!"

"Bye, devil," Simbol yelled.

Then with as much force as she attempted the other night, Simbol slammed the door.

"All your life we've been telling you to stop slamming that door. This is the one time that it's alright," Mr. King gladly proclaimed.

"And when did you become so ghetto, Simbol?" Divine asked with laughter in her throat.

"Girl, sometimes you got to let Simbolaqueesha out cause she can get some stuff done. Don't make me pop my chewing gum and my neck. Enough said, Boo."

Simbol acted as ghetto as possible which was hilarious yet fitting at this particular moment.

The three sisters high fived each other signifying a job well done. They had killed the enemy with kindness while setting her up for failure. The three of them surrounded their dad with a hug.

"You couldn't get rid of us if you tried."

Hugging his daughters almost crying, Alto was very grateful that God knew how to answer prayers. He felt so free. God had delivered him from his past mistakes or at least the one that he thought he had made. Thinking deeply on that caused him to start laughing a deep bellowing laugh.

The girls stood back looking puzzled, as they had never seen their daddy this joyous before.

"What's so funny?" Divine asked.

He continued to laugh so hard that he bent over slapping his knees.

"Dad sure is tickled. I want to know," Simbol whined.

Catching his breath and straightening his body, he began to explain what had got him so caught up in laughter.

"It went through my mind of how when I thought I had cheated on Pastoria, I ran straight to the church and got saved. Had it not been for Beatrice telling that lie then I probably wouldn't be saved today. I wonder what the devil thinks about that. God tricked him again. You can't tell me that God won't use a devil to drive his people to church."

He erupted into laughing again but this time everybody joined in.

When they had gotten finished basking in victory, the girls started to clean up the dishes. He asked Vera to walk with him. They went outside to sit on the porch.

"Have a seat, Vera."

Vera did exactly what he asked. She was no stranger to this porch as she sat in her favorite chair here. Rocking back and forth, she thought about her sweet friend, Pastoria. They had shared decades knowing each other but it took the both of them having to go onto dialysis to actually bond closer than sisters do.

"Vera, I sure do thank you for saving the day. You just don't know what that means to me. I didn't want to do anything that was going to make grief harder for my girls."

"You got some sweet girls. They're a lot like their mama."

Alto thought on that for a moment smiling. "Yes they are."

"She told me to make sure that y'all be alright."

"And you have held up to your end of the bargain. You just don't know how much we appreciate you. But I do have one question for you."

Vera stopped rocking and turned her body to look at Alto. She already had a feeling what he was going to say, so she answered it for him.

"You want to know when I told Pastoria. Two weeks before that night, the church had come by passing out tracks and inviting us to church. You remember that ol' raggedy duplex that my family stayed on one side and Beatrice and her cousins stayed on the other?"

Briefly remembering, Alto nodded in agreement.

"Well the church came by and Pastoria was the one who talked to me. She was just as kind as she wanted to be not even looking down on me when she found out that I had been fast and done broke my leg. It ain't like it is today. These girls go around with they stomachs poked out with no husbands and don't feel an ounce of shame." Vera's voice heightened almost squeaking.

"But I was ashamed. So Pastoria told me about how before she married you that y'all messed up too but you just got married before she started showing."

Alto nodded his head smiling at the memory.

"To make a long story short, she encouraged my heart so, kept checking on me and the baby. She even brought him a toy. So when I saw what Beatrice was up to and with who, I looked through that crack in the wall all night long praying that God not let nothing happen cause of yo' wife sake. I kept looking and never saw nothing. Then when you woke up, I heard exactly what she said to you. You were so shocked. You stumbled your way out of there and you never came back."

"I sure didn't. I was scared." Alto hung his head from the shame of the memory. "But when did you tell Pastoria?"

"I told her probably about a month after it happened. My conscience ate me up so bad. She brought the baby some milk and I told her every bit of it."

Alto looked at her intensely. "Did it hurt her?"

"The part that hurt her was that she thought that Beatrice was her friend. I think that she cleaved to you more knowing that you didn't do anything."

"I wonder why she never said anything. She didn't even let on that she knew."

"What she told me was just what you said in there earlier. The devil caused her prayer to be answered. You ran to the church. She was afraid that if she told you that she knew that you didn't do anything then you might backslide."

Alto shook his head. He thought about all the money that he could have saved if Pastoria would have told him. Then he changed his thinking by realizing that the value of his soul was worth far more than what had been blackmailed from him by Beatrice.

"She's right. I probably would have. Pastoria knew best. I thank God for my wife. And I thank God for her having a real friend."

When he looked at Vera again, she was standing with her hand extended. Tears began to fill his eyes when he saw his name in his wife's handwriting. He took the letter carefully never taking his eyes from it.

Vera walked away leaving Alto to read in peace. As she crossed the threshold entering the house, she looked back smiling knowing her job of keeping this family together was done.

Alto,

My beloved husband. I thank God for how you took care of me and our beautiful girls. I could not have asked for a better husband. Even though everything wasn't always perfect according to someone else's standards, it was perfect to me. I love you with every part of my being; heart, mind and soul. What we have is magical.

I know that you're going to be alright in time. The girls are too. However, they are going to need you like never before to guide them and direct them in the right way. I know they are grown but they will always be my babies.

I know you call me a busybody. Man, I'm going to bite you! ☺ But you have to be the busybody now when it comes to our daughters. I'm not so concerned about Divine, she has Gerald and the boys. But you make sure that you be there for her if the time comes. That's our firstborn. The seed of our little slip up. If I had to do it all over again, I would.

Simbol definitely needs you. She is soft as mush on the inside but super strong on the outside because of what she went through with that abusive man. It might be a little tough getting her to open up her heart to love again but I already got him lined up for her. Lane is a good man and you know it. He is perfect for her. He's strong enough to handle her if he can get next to her.

Now our baby girl is going to be a special case. She's so busy trying to be right with God that she doesn't realize that God wants her to be with the right one. Christian is the one for her. The poor child is trying to keep herself busy doing everything everywhere because she's trying to smother the hormones God gave her. She needs Christian so desperately. I know he will make her his wife this time. He'll make her a great husband just like you were for me. Lane knows how to get in contact with him. You need to get them to communicate. As the young people say, "make it happen."

I know that you are going to take care of our girls and they are going to take care of you. I wish I could be there but I fulfilled our vows; until death do we part. I was happily your wife for my life. I'll see you whenever your time comes. I so love you, Alto. Thank you for a beautiful life on earth,

Pastoria

Although the letter had ended, he wanted more. "Oh, Pastoria, I so love you too."

Kenali eavesdropped on the conversation between her dad and Ms. Vera. She walked away wondering with all the similarities why her story couldn't end like that. This thing with Christian was getting so complicated and frustrating all at the same time. Her emotions were out of control. She just wanted him as far away from her as possible.

Then she thought back to the letter her mom had written to her and how it went on and on about Christian being the right one.

Mama, you didn't know all this craziness was going to happen.

Kenali had to get out of there to go somewhere she could think.

Hurrying up to finish cleaning, she did not even involve herself too much in the gloating conversation that Divine and Simbol had going on. This was a time she should have been celebrating this victorious day instead her spirit was muffled.

"Well, we're all done. I'm going to step out for a little while."

"Where are you going," Simbol asked being nosy.

"To my little spot in the woods. I'll be back in a couple of hours."

"Ok. You be careful out there by yourself."

"I will."

With that, Kenali got into her car driving more in a hurry than she did last night when she had to go check on her house. This was even more crucial. She had no peace.

When she passed by her house seeing how it had been psychotically decorated, she cringed. More anger had been added to her ill mood. Then she thought about how she yelled at Christian. Part of her said, "way to go, sister" while the other side said, "shame on you."

Kenali had arrived at her destination. She remembered all the times that she and Christian would come out here to have a picnic or just to sit to inhale its beauty. An oasis is what they called it back then.

She walked the trail until it dumped her full fledge into this hidden paradise. Immediately she went to the water's edge scooping up her dress so that it would not get wet. She stooped down to run her fingers through the water. The temperature of the water was perfect for those that took swims in natural waters. For herself, it was oceans or pools, no rivers or ponds.

Looking at her rippled reflection, she correlated it with her present life—it wasn't clear. She thought about all she had been through these last few days rating each of them based on severity. Of course, losing her mother was number one followed by...she couldn't come up with a clear number two. The Beatrices and the Julias and the vandalism would share a three way tie for second place. They each were just too new for her. Christian coming in at third wasn't to say that his part in adding to her heaviness was insignificant; he was just familiar.

A gentle breeze blew through the long blades of grass; the tree leaves waved in applause. Any other time this would bring her so much peace. However, today was different. Her stubborn troubles just refuse to be evicted. Getting rid of Beatrice should have brought a release but it didn't. It just made her realize that when you're dealing with a greatly multiplied sorrow, the releasing of one thing doesn't guarantee relief.

Kenali then cried thinking about the last meal with her mom that she missed. It seemed the more things she tried to get rid of the more that found an entrance to come torment her.

"Mama, if I could have that day again…"

Not even finishing the sentence, her heart completed that it would be different. Despite the encouragement others, her mother included, had given her, that particular day would always haunt her.

She found her way through teary eyes, to sit underneath the gazebo. Sitting in the wooden swing, she held her head back allowing the tears to coat the back of her neck. It was slightly dizzying looking up at the roof with sunlight peeping in between the slats of each plank.

Closing her eyes, with her arms lifelessly by her sides, she rocked allowing the swing to whisk her through the air. Her eyes burned from holding in the tears, which escaped anyway when a surplus of them gathered.

Kenali needed a way to release this pain. Capturing the scripture in her mind that God would not put more on you than you can bear, only made her inability to find peace seem as if God thought she was stronger than she actually were.

Not getting much sleep after his nightmare, Christian sat in the antique wicker rocker the remainder of the night staring out the window. Not only was his body exhausted but so was his heart and mind.

These last few days have been one for the books.

He knew that between now and his flight early Monday morning, he was going to have to be sharp. His office called him rerouting his travels to Tennessee. He was going to secure an advertising client at a mountain resort in Nashville.

Had things been working out for him, he would have turned the short flight into a road trip for him and Kenali. Right now, he knew they were over.

Maybe it was good for him to be here after all. Now he could release her from his mind. Retrieving the ring from his pocket, he placed the open box on the window seal. The sunlight kissed it and the diamond winked back.

Christian walked away from it, to begin his day, his life without Kenali. After that horror show in his sleep last night, he definitely made up his mind that he needed to start going back to church. He figured that's what he got for sleeping in his mama's bed. Of course, she was going to make him realize that he turned his back on God for a woman that turned her back on him. How juvenile he had been.

When he reached Lane's house, he discussed his new life plan with him. He could tell Lane was pleased.

"About time!" Lane dramatically exclaimed. "I knew you were thick headed as a child but dang as a man also. I kept wondering when you were going to get it."

"You still got jokes," Christian smiled back already expecting this reaction from Lane.

Lane hugged him pounding him on the back. "Laughter does good like medicine. I can have you over medicated and you ain't gotta spend a dime. All cause I'm free cuz and you are too now."

Lane celebrated by pounding his fist in his hand. It was if he was so happy that he couldn't contain it.

"Yeah cuz! I mean you're gonna make mistakes cause you just starting but just watch how much better your life is gonna get overall."

The more excited Lane got, the better Christian felt on the inside. It was almost as if the horrific past few days and the nightmare was a necessary door to get him to this point. He truly hoped that something good was going to make his life better.

They made plans to go to church on Sunday. He already knew of a church in New York that was only a couple of blocks away from where he lived. Christian almost couldn't believe it; he had to give up, letting everything go, just to feel this kind of relief. He could only think of how he should have done this sooner.

Preparing to leave, saying his see you later to Lane, Christian's phone went off displaying a number that he was definitely familiar with. After he hung up the phone, he couldn't help but to think that God works really fast.

❧✦✦✦✦✦✦☙

Christian rang the doorbell with caution; the last time Simbol was about to scald him with hot water. He could see through the glass that Simbol was coming to answer the door; luckily she had nothing in her hands. Nevertheless, he prepared himself to run, duck or whatever he had to for safety reasons.

"Hey, Christian. Come on in," Simbol gleefully spoke moving to the side to allow him to enter.

Christian was nervous and confused. He now knew that Simbol had to have split personalities.

"Hey, Simbol."

He didn't risk calling her Ms. Sassy. She could have a hidden blade in her bra for all he knew.

"Daddy's out on the porch." She nodded her head in that direction. Then she turned to skip up the stairs. "You know your way around the house."

He watched her hop up the stairs with so much spring in her step that he wondered what happened to her. She had to know something he didn't. Was Mr. King about to kill him for taking Kenali through the ringer emotionally? That had to be it. His feet did not know whether to turn to run out the door or walk to his demise. Before he could make a decision, it was made for him.

"Oh, hey, Christian. I thought I heard the doorbell. Come on out here." Mr. King waved for him to come where he was.

Christian obeyed. He then went outside doing everything he was told to do. Have a seat; he sat. Here's something to drink; he drank. Then he realized that Mr. King was not trying to kill him but in fact was on his side.

This God thing is off the chain.

"I want you to talk to my daughter. She might be a little mad right now. Be gentle with her. She might feel

❧┼☙

199

that everything is against her and I can't blame her for thinking like that. I sat back looking and her load has been heavier than the rest of ours."

Mr. King stopped talking taking a sip of his deliciously cold lemonade. The ice cubes tinged against the glass, which sweated from the Alabama humidity. After he placed the glass down onto its coaster, he shook the water from his hand.

"Now I'm going to tell you to do something that might be hard for you. She's probably going to want to hit something or somebody. Let her hit you. But you have my permission to hold her tight until she stops fighting. Christian, she got to get this stuff out of her and if you love her like my wife said that you do, then you will do or go through whatever it takes until she releases it."

Mr. King stood up leaving Christian with one final nugget before walking away.

"You're a good man. You remind me of myself. But whatever you do, don't bring my baby girl anymore hurt. Handle your business with that other woman. Do what you got to do to make it right."

With that, he went down the three steps from the porch into the yard. Locking his hands together behind his back, Mr. King slowly walked until he disappeared into rows of trees.

Christian jumped to his feet dialing Kenali's number. No answer. When he turned to walk into the house, he saw a note attached to the door on the inside. He walked through the door retrieving the note.

Kenali said she was going to a little spot in the woods. You might know where that is.

Don't hurt my sister or I got something extra hot for you.

-Ms. Sassy

Snatching the note from the door, he ran through the house, dove into his car, and drove as if his life depended on it. It was almost dark and he figured that if she left there he would be playing phone tag to no avail.

When he reached the spot, their oasis, her car was parked on the side of the road. Standing at the end of the trail still concealed by the trees, he spied on her. She was lying in the grass in a fetal position crying. Her body was jerking frantically. His heart ached. Mr. King was right; this was going to be hard.

He touched her arm and she jumped backing away from him. She was frightened.

Bad move Christian, he thought.

"I'm sorry. I didn't mean to scare you."

Her face was wet with tears. She harshly wiped her face.

"Well you did!" she yelled.

She came to her feet dusting her dress off.

"Why would you sneak up behind someone like that anyway?" Her anger had surfaced in a way he had never seen.

"Look, Kenali, just calm down." He kept his composure to lead her the same way although it seemed to aggravate her even more.

"Calm down? Calm down! You calm down!"

"I am calm."

"I know why you're calm," she yelled approaching him. "It's because you're bringing drama into everybody else's life." Kenali released the first blow to his chest. She was definitely stronger than she looked.

"I didn't mean for any of—"

"You never mean for anything to happen." A right and a left hook followed her words into his chest.

That's why Mr. King warned this was going to be hard. He must have known Kenali has been strength training.

She swiftly swiped at the fresh tears that streamed down her face. "You knew my mama had died but you came down here with that crazy b—" She interrupted the words from becoming profane although she was mad enough to cuss. "Crazy person following behind you. Why would you do me like that? You can't love me." She pounded him with every word.

"I do love you, Kenali."

She never stopped to hear him. She was still enraged, which was doing her more harm than good.

"I feel so stupid for still loving you."

She cried so hard that she momentarily ceased from breathing. She was becoming hysterical almost to the point of having a panic attack.

Christian had to do something, remembering Mr. King's instructions, he pulled her to his chest wrapping his arms around her. She struggled to resist. She kicked at his shins. His heart grieved to see her like this.

"Let me go! Why can't you just stay away from me?"

There were no signs of Kenali calming down anytime soon. Christian could not let her continue on this magnitude so he acted on impulse. He kept one arm around her, reaching to grab her face with the other. Pulling her chin up, he planted a kiss on her. Her lips were salty from the tears.

Kissing her, he felt the twinge of the past few days' pains, frustrations, and disappointments hot on her lips.

She struggled not to release it. Her uncontrollable sobbing continued. He could feel the trembling of her throat in his hand. She stopped kicking yet she still slightly squirmed beneath his grip. Kenali began yielding to him; she kissed him back.

His wanting to help her turned the tables transforming into the stored up desire from the past three years being fueled by her response to him. Next, he did the only thing that the man inside him knew to do; he made love to her with all the familiarity of their past. They were surrounded by darkness in their own oasis gripped by enough failure to light the sky.

Kenali walked into her father's house immediately going up the stairs. Simbol recognizing something was not right about her, followed.

"I better not need to get that hot water," she mumbled to herself.

Not even knocking, she entered into Kenali's room behind her.

"What's going on?"

Kenali looked blank. Simbol didn't like that look, never did. That meant Kenali was beating herself up on the inside. Kenali's eyebrows wrinkled. Simbol walked into the bathroom to get a box of tissues simply because she knew that Kenali was about to explode in tears.

"I should have never told him where she was. He better watch his back," Simbol mumbled at an octave only she could hear.

Reentering the room, Kenali was still standing there straight as a board. Simbol pulled two tissues from the box handing them to Kenali who in turn looked down at her hand doing what the sight of the tissues instigated. She let out a squeal so painful that Simbol reasoned that it was going to be hot oil instead of water. She had to ensure the pain stuck to Christian for a while.

∽｜∾

She held her sister allowing her to cry on her shoulder feeling the heat of her tears fall upon her bare arms.

"Don't worry Kenali. I'm going to get Christian for doing this." Simbol was firm in her speech. She meant every word of what she said.

Kenali defended Christian. "It's not his fault."

Simbol failed to understanding what was going on. "Well, what happened?"

Kenali stepped back sobbing in spurts. Every time she tried to speak, she halted her words. She didn't know if she could tell anyone of her failure; tell of her recent sin. When she blurted it out there was no taking it back.

"My flesh wanted it. I wanted it. Then it went too far and I didn't want to stop. I started yelling at him and kicking him and hitting him and then it…it just happened."

Kenali was talking mostly with her hands which was confusing Simbol.

From thinking that she knew what Kenali was talking about her eyes widened.

"Oh, my God! What did you do? Did you kill Christian?"

Kenali looked at Simbol, paused from her crying, wondering what she had said that would make her think she killed Christian.

"No! I messed up. I didn't mean to let my guard down. Having sex was so far from my mind." Kenali plopped down on the bed hanging her head down.

After a moment, Simbol started laughing.

"Whew! That's all. That's a light affliction. I thought we was going to have to dig a hole to hide the body. Dude is six-foot-four. We were going to need a backhoe for a hole that big."

It was safe for Kenali to do what she had been thinking about for years; write Simbol off as crazy.

"Simbol, did you hear what I said?"

"Yes. You said you had sex." Simbol shrugged as if it meant nothing to her.

"I had sex, Simbol. I messed up. I had been abstinent for over three years and planned on being so until I got married."

"Ok. Did you plan it?"

"No. God no!"

"Are you planning on doing it later on?"

"No. I already feel horrible."

"Then Kenali, what's the problem? You're a grown woman. Are you forgetting who you are?"

Kenali looked at Simbol one hundred percent confused.

"Ok. Maybe I'm not saying it like I'm thinking it. Kenali, you're saved by His grace. That doesn't mean that you are not going to make a mistake. When we fall to temptation, then we ask forgiveness for yielding. Then you ask God to help keep you from going back into the same thing."

After thinking on it for a while, Kenali conjured up a rebuttal.

"I've been abstinent since I broke up with Christian. Besides, I have resisted other men all this time."

"Like who?"

"Ronnie."

"Ewww. That's easy. He's ugly as sin."

"Carmichael."

"Is he still missing a couple of teeth?"

"Johnathon."

"Broke." Simbol exhaled harshly. "Look, you can keep coming up with these names looking for a way to punish yourself but there's no point in it. Don't get me wrong. I'm not saying that you have a ticket to do anything you want cause you don't. You made an honest mistake and with everything that's going on, the last thing you need to do is refuse the forgiveness that's waiting for you."

Kenali took a moment to understand that her sister was right. After shooing Simbol's crazy behind out of her room, she did just that. She asked for forgiveness and felt a peace that she really needed. After showering, she got into the bed letting their conversation go through her head. Laughter erupted from her. Carmichael was still missing his teeth.

Christian paced back and forth in front of the fireplace. He intertwined his fingers together at the base of his neck, clenching his teeth together, he yelled at himself.

"So stupid!"

Christian swung his fist through the air with great force. Had someone been on the receiving end, a trip to the hospital would have been inevitable.

He was having a fit all by himself. Trying to figure out how he keeps goofing up, he exhaled and shook his head.

"I can't win for losing. That's a bad move, Christian."

The only thing he could do to defend himself was to remember that having sex with Kenali was never his motive. He had never seen her so hysterical and it seemed as if she had no control over it. He sat on the couch with his elbows on his knees and his head in his hands.

Not knowing what to do to fix it since everything that he attempted to make right only got worse with her being on the receiving end of the chaos, he searched his mind for something in his heart. Then he knew exactly what it was.

"God, if you give me another chance, I promise, I'll make it right this time."

☞ | ☜

This was going to be another sleepless night but it was going to be worth it all. With so much planning to do, sleep was the only thing to eliminate.

As soon as the sun came up, he shot out the door to get this day started right. He made all the necessary phone calls and met with the appropriate people that could help him make his last day in town perfect. Sunday was going to be envied by the rest of the days of the week because of what he was working so hard to make happen.

Now that everything was set and in place, he only had one more person to call; Kenali. Actually, he didn't call her. He opted out to send her a text message for the one reason that he could not masque the joy in his voice. She of all people would have known that he was up to something. Whipping the cell out of his pocket, he put the final thing on his list in motion.

Can I take you on a date Sunday morning to church? I'll pick you up at 8:30. Let me make it right. I love you Kenali.

Sunday morning came swiftly, which was good since he felt like a kid on Christmas morning. He was ready to tear into this day and all that it offered him. Christian prepared in a way that he never has before.

Choosing to wear white linen pants and shirt both piped in black chording matched with a pair of white, square toed Kenneth Cole crocodiles that had a black metallic buckle offset to the outer part of his foot. Looking in the full length mirror, he was confident. Christian felt that his situation had flipped; he was now on top of the world instead of the other way around.

"Brother, you look good," he encouraged himself.

He made one last stop by his mom's room before exiting the house. He picked up his favorite girl and she was even more beautiful. He was glad Simbol was able to convince her to wear white. She had on a long white flowing maxi dress with a silver link chain draped around her waist. Christian could not resist thinking that Kenali looked like a daughter of God. At this point he fully understood that he had to belong to Him to have her.

"We're matching," she said oblivious of his hand in it.

Even since the other day, the day of their falling, she was completely different. He knew that she was going to be alright by the way that she looked up at him when she sat into the car. When he closed the door, he walked around the car with a renewed heart. His stride changed confidently.

All during the church service, he was ready for his next move. When he felt it getting closer, he nervously bounced his leg causing Kenali to put her hand on his knee. If she only knew what he was about to do, then her knees would bounce too. Then the moment came; the pastor made the announcement.

"Would anyone like to start again today? Will there be one that would like to give their life to the Lord?"

When he stood up, with nothing but shock in her face, Kenali followed him with her eyes. Christian couldn't resist the urge to look back at her. He winked. Simbol tapped her on her shoulder while Lane leaned forward to whisper in her ear.

"God didn't make you wait for nothing."

Kenali blushed.

Christian went through the prayer of redemption and repeated after the minister until he belonged completely to God both in his heart and by the power of his words.

Kenali hugged him with so much joy. Lane and Simbol congratulated him before going their separate ways. Christian felt like a completely different man although he still wasn't finished.

"I want to take you somewhere. Do you trust me?"

His voice was full of an excitement that matched his eyes.

Wondering of where he could possibly want to take her, she agreed.

"Then put this on."

Christian handed her a black strip of cloth.

"It's not my size. Just a teeny bit too small," she joked.

He laughed at her while she put on the blindfold. Knowing that she knew the area like the back of her hand, he took unnecessary turns just to confuse her. When they arrived, he carried her to her destination. Getting into the right position, he placed her in the center of the gazebo and pulled the blindfold from her eyes.

She looked around seeing that she was in their oasis. Her hands covered her mouth when she inhaled the beauty of her surroundings. Her family and friends were all standing around flashing smiles as white as their clothing. The area had been transformed with lights hanging from the trees, tables draped with white linens blowing in the delicate breezes. Centerpieces of white pompoms with sparkly jewels affixed on them graced the tables. There was soft music playing enhancing the magic of the moment. Was the Heaven on Earth?

This was so beautiful that Kenali didn't know whether to laugh or to cry. When she looked around at Christian, he was on bended knee with a hand extended out. Finally noticing what was at the end of his hand, she responded before he even asked.

"Yes!"

He stood victoriously picking her up above his head kissing her the right way this time.

He had loved her for as long as he could remember. Having his special girl in his arms and heart, he tuned out the applause. He now knew what Lane meant when he said God was going to make his life good. This moment exceeded that. It was the best.

The elderly couple that owned this spot came to congratulate them. The elderly man winked at him leaning in to Christian.

"I didn't know that you had the writer of the Love Is poem. Now that you know what love is, you can't go wrong."

Christian was amazed that his favorite girl, Kenali King, was the one that contained the wisdom that is far beyond her age about the workings of love.

It all made sense to him that night, when they went to Spoken Café. Just from the mere entrance of her, the crowd of her poetic peers began to shout, "Love Is." With the added nudging from the M.C., she complied with their request.

As Kenali took the stage, the audience quieted down to reveal the jazzy feel of the music. You would have actually thought that she was about to sing but she was about to walk in her calling which was flowing words. Before she began, she looked to see that the group she came with had seated themselves close to the seat she and Christian had their first of many conversations. While looking at the excitement on his face, she began speaking.

"Hello, everyone. I heard your request for me to do Love Is. But before I begin I want you all to know that the inspiration for Love Is sits right back there very close to the area in which we had our first real conversation."

The crowd all looked back to see a bashful version of Christian.

"This is Love Is."

Looking back at the musicians, Kenali said, "Could I get something slow?"

People settled themselves down so there would be no movement that would cause them to miss anything. They hung onto her every word. The music swayed them; Kenali's voice soothed them.

"Love is when two touch and agree upon the same heartbeat.

Not caring who is the rib or who has to be put to sleep.

As long as this love continues to exist.

As long as the two continue to persist.

For how can two walk together unless they agree?

Standing in ordained love beneath God Almighty."

Listening to her words, Christian thought that maybe she knew this day was going to happen whenever she wrote the poem.

"Love is the release of breath from one's soul to another's heart,

Because God first demonstrated love from the very start.

We have been created to duplicate a love so extraordinary.

A love so pure that the songs cheerfully come from the beaks of Canaries.

Love is the completing of each other's sentences and the discernment of thoughts.

Not having to say a word about how a love like this can't be bought.

After an argument, the sun doesn't go down before you utter, 'I'm sorry for this.'

And the reply is always I happily extend to you forgiveness."

When Kenali spoke this line on forgiveness, her spirit bowed to the recognition of its power. She forgave herself for pushing Christian away. She forgave herself for not having the last meal with her mom and she forgave herself for falling. She was not going to make Jesus' work be in vain.

"Love is being just as compatible as the paper and pen,
Disliking the time that separates you from being back together again.
The wind at your back from the angel's wings put swiftness to your feet,
Interlocking in a sweet embrace to bring upon separation a much needed defeat whenever you meet.
Love is looking in the mirror to see your mate's vision
Willing to help build their dream without knowing every decision.
Love is the ability to release oneself before your very own eyes
To form strength in the bonds of compromise.
Love is sometimes really complicated,
But for some reason we continue to strive to duplicate it."

Christian knew all too well how complicated love could be. If he had not taken the elderly man's advice to fight for Kenali, he would not have been able to walk into his now.

He took notice that Kenali was digging into her flow. He wanted so much to lock eyes with her but they were closed softly as if she was reading the words on the back of her eyelids.

"Love is loving another like God loves the church as He looks down.
Love is constantly offering an upside down frown.
Love is something more often lived than learned.
Love is the very feeling that our hearts yearn.
Love is a noun, an adjective, and a verb.

214

Love is an emotion that is best not disturbed.
Love is always awake therefore never finding sleep.
Simply put, Love is just deep."

Cheers erupted from the audience in the vocal sense as well as the snapping of fingers. By the time Kenali opened her eyes, Christian was standing at the bottom of the stage. He was feeling so good that he mouthed to her I love you and yelled to the audience.

"She said yes!"

Once again, the crowd applauded this time with a standing ovation. Grabbing her around her waist, he took her into his arms. He just couldn't stop kissing her. Maybe it was a way of making up for lost time.

Julia exploded out the exit not believing what her ears just heard.

"Get out the way!" she unleashed onto someone outside almost bulldozing them over.

"Did he say she said yes?" she screamed in the alleyway as she walked to her car.

Half of her mind told her to go back in there and slap those silly smiles right off both of their faces. But the other part told her to keep her cool. Somehow, she dismissed the calmer voice to pay close attention to the more chaotic one.

"Who do they think they are?" Julia fumed.

She made her way back to the café. Now standing in the doorway, she sought her not so favorite couple. She spotted Kenali crossing the room alone. Looking to where she came from, Julia noticed Christian and company sitting at a table exchanging laughter. She wickedly winced before slithering behind Kenali.

Seeing Kenali entering the restroom, Julia hesitated to think of what she would do. Then impulse took over as she pushed the door open with so much force it startled the woman standing at the sink washing her hands. Noticing the demented look on Julia's face, the woman rushed her task as she wanted no part of anything that was about to go down.

Julia leaned against the countertop with her arms folded waiting for Kenali to come out of the stall. She could hear her humming which was like nails on a chalkboard to Julia. Finally, Kenali came out with her head down as she was adjusting her clothing. When she looked up directly into the flaming eyes of Julia, she slightly jerked.

"Did I catch you off guard?" Julia's voice was as cold as ice.

Gaining recognition of who she was, Kenali became very perturbed.

"You just look different with clothes on. Maybe if you had a can of spray paint, I might have noticed you quicker."

With caution yet full of boldness, Kenali approached the sink to wash her hands. Julia looked her up and down.

"I see that congratulations are in order. It must feel good to steal another woman's man?"

Julia rolled her eyes pursing her lips out with disgust.

"How could I steal what you never had? Step into reality Julia. Now, I don't know what happened between you and Christian in the past but you need to leave the past where it is and live for today."

"Don't try to tell me how to live my life!" she yelled.

Julia's words matched her emotions of quick anger. She only paused to look at someone entering the restroom.

"You don't know anything about me! As a matter of fact, I know about you and I can't stand witches like you. You get a good man and you throw him away because you don't want him anymore. Then a woman like me comes along, encourages, and nourishes his mind back to strength and then you decide that you want him back."

"That's where you got it all twisted. It didn't go down like that and I don't have to explain to you either. I got something for that man that you will never have or understand and that is real love. I love him and no matter what you think of me, you can never love him as much as I do."

With the finishing of her sentence, Kenali turned to walk out the bathroom.

She walked just a little piece down the hallway and was immediately caught by Julia who grabbed her arm with so much force that Kenali spun around.

"Don't you walk away from me!" Julia harshly spoke through clenched teeth.

Kenali's eyebrow raised. She squared herself face-to-face with Julia. Her words were slow but firm.

"If you ever put your hands on me again—"

"What? What are you going to do? Go tell Christian."

"Go tell Christian? I'm grown. I don't have to run to tell anybody anything. I can handle my own."

Their audience had increased. There were people either coming to or from the restrooms that decided to wait for these two women to get done before passing by.

"Yeah. I bet you can. We're going to see." Julia fumed back.

"Julia, you need to get some help. If you think I'm about to be out here shaming myself fighting with you about God knows what, you got another thing coming," Kenali paused briefly thinking of everything Julia had done. "Now, I have every right to want to knock you out, but I'm not about to stoop to your crazy level. Girl, you need some prayer!"

At the mentioning of prayer, Julia's level of anger reached an all-time high, which was evident as she paced back and forth. She couldn't contain her emotions any longer. As Kenali walked away from her once more, that was the same as throwing gas on hellfire.

"Pray? I don't need your prayers. Save them for yourself. You're going to need them when I get finished with you."

With that announcement, Julia began charging towards Kenali who then turned to face her. Before Julia could reach Kenali, the heel on her stiletto gave way sending her sprawling onto the floor.

A quick wave of sympathy flashed over Kenali towards Julia until she remembered how torturous she had made her life recently. It suddenly dissipated.

"I'm going to pray that you get up with enough dignity and sense to know that you're fighting a losing battle."

Kenali finally dismissed herself from the scene she had not invited into her life.

Julia pounded her fist on the floor while the onlookers watched in disbelief.

"Girl, you need to do better," said a woman who was a witness to the entire event.

As one of the young men tried to be a gentleman and help her up, she nastily signified that she didn't want his help. He then turned on her to begin taunting her so much that she hurriedly picked herself up with the wounded shoe in her hand to scamper out of the cafe.

Julia was angrier than she was when she first came out. At this point, she didn't know which was worse, hearing the announcement of the engagement or falling at Kenali's feet. Inside her mind, she just knew that it couldn't end like this. She had to make them both pay.

She made a pick up before going back to her room. Rationalizing that she needed this hit to be able to keep her from going back to Spoken Café wreaking havoc, she allowed the drug to do what it was designed to do.

Feeling its affects shortly after consumption, she leveled out beginning to think deeply. Her mind went back to when her friend advised her not to start back again; getting clean would be more hell than the first time. She was right. Now that she had started back, it was hard to deny wanting it the very next day.

She picked up the phone; her mind was made up.

"Before you say anything, I just wanted to say you were a great friend who looked out for me through thick and thin," Julia's words were slurring.

"Julia, what's wrong? Please don't tell me you did that."

There was silence. She heard Julia whimpering.

"All I wanted was his heart. Why couldn't he want me back? But no! He had to want her. Even when he was with me, it was about her."

Julia paused from talking to cry. That was the opportunity her friend needed to jump into the conversation.

"Julia, there are other men out there better than Christian. You can be really happy if you—"

"They're not him!" she screamed into the receiver before calming her tone. "They're not him."

"Just come home. I can help you," her friend strongly pleaded.

"I can't go through that hell of trying to get clean again. Oh, no. New York will never see me again. I was calling to say goodbye."

"So you're just going to live down there?"

"No. Where I'm going, Christian and I will be together—forever."

Taking a much earlier flight, Julia was already outside the airport holding a sign up with Christian's name. She saw him before he spotted her. His body language showed how reluctant he was to come her way.

"Hey. What happened to Spencer?" Christian asked expecting someone else.

"He's in the hospital. They think it might be a real bad case of food poisoning. I'm parked over here," Julia was robotic.

Christian put his bag into the trunk, then strapped himself into the passenger side. He thought of how she wasn't as talkative as usual but that was good for his sake. He knew that she was most likely embarrassed about what happened last night.

"Do you have the address?"

"Yes!" she snapped.

"Whoa. You don't have to bite my head off. I was just asking."

"Yeah, whatever," she jerked the car into traffic.

"Look, if your attitude is about what happened then—"

"Hey! What's done is done. This is business as usual." Julia had to cut him off. His voice was irritation to her eardrums.

He momentarily thought about what she said. "Alright. Great. I agree. Business as usual."

Then he tuned his attention into the work in his briefcase. He scanned over his presentation notes that was definitely going to wheel this client in. After all, he had been working with this resort for a few months now and if they wanted him to come down, then in his experience, they were ready to sign on the dotted line.

After what seemed like a long time of driving, he noticed that they were in the mountains which was the biggest part about this trip that he didn't like especially with Julia behind the wheel speeding.

His phone, which was inside his briefcase, lit up displaying a text message.

> Hey Christian. Where are you? I'm waiting by the curb.
> Spencer

Christian gulped hard. His mind flashed to the movies in which people had been abducted by a deranged person who they thought was cool with everything. He now knew how they felt.

Not knowing what else to do, he sent a reply. Maybe this was a joke.

> I thought you were in the hospital. Julia picked me up.

Please let him say this was a joke. Otherwise, he could not think of what to do. The car was going too fast to jump out. Besides there was nothing but cliffs on the side; he was bound to roll off.

Another text message came in.

> Julia??? She quit.

Christian's breathing became irregular. Loosening his tie, he looked at her from the corner of his eyes.

"What's the matter, Christian? Spencer looking for you?" Her laugh was deep and evil.

"Look, why don't you just pull over?"

"You know, that's the nicest you've talked to me in a while. But too late now."

"It's never too late, Julia," Christian's voice was shaky.

He felt hot all over as if he knew death was impending.

She pressed the accelerator harder. He gripped the door handle.

"It is for me and you. Oh yeah, I guess congratulations are in order for your marriage that *would* have been coming up. Love is." Julia sucked her teeth snapping her fingers in mock of last night's events. The more she mimicked the more perturbed she became. "You're such and idiot!"

"Julia, come on, I mean—"

"Shut up! You wasn't telling me to come on when you were so busy yelling out, 'she said yes'. And then she had the nerve to embarrass me!"

Julia was heaving noticeably with her chest drastically rising and dropping.

"Since you love her so much, get her on the phone."

Thinking about her request, he denied. "No. I won't."

"If you don't get her on the phone, I promise I'll run this car over the cliff."

"Look, Julia, we can work this out," Christian begged.

His stomach felt the same as it did in his nightmare. This was not good at all. He had never been this close to the receiving end of death. There was nothing he could do at this point other than pray that God would help him.

"Do it now, Christian!" she yelled so loudly it rattled her voice box.

Christian's hands shook terribly. He was stuck between a rock and a hard place, literally. He dialed the number, putting the phone to his ear. He felt regret although the hope that Julia wouldn't kill them both was slightly still alive.

"Hey, honey," Kenali's voice was still sweet to him even in a deadly situation.

"I will always love you." He spoke through the tears in his throat. As the engine revved more, all hope disappeared. He knew Julia was going to attempt to kill him.

"Christian, what's wrong," he heard Kenali say while the phone was being ripped from his face.

"Christian's going to die today. And it's all your fault."

Despite Christian's scrambling to get the phone, Julia held it on the other side of her face. He could not believe that one more thing was being added to Kenali's plate of heaviness.

"Yes, all your fault! All you had to do was release his heart but you're so greedy. But guess what? Just like you said last night about love being deep, so is this cliff. I got him forever. I win. Now pray about that!"

Julia threw the phone into the back seat and jerked the car to send it over the cliff.

Christian grabbed the steering wheel to turn it the other way before it went over but either way was bad. It went across the road scrubbing against jagged rock only to bounce back across the street breaking through the guardrail sending the car over head first.

He always wanted his dreams to come true; just not that particular one.

KENALI 6 Months Later

There's a saying that goes something like, whatever doesn't kill you will only make you stronger. Kenali wasn't sure if she wanted to adopt that theory. As she looked back into six months ago, she understood what God meant when he told Eve that her sorrow would become greatly multiplied. Kenali had lived it outside of the Garden of Eden, which made it hell on earth.

During that time, Kenali had to recognize the three things that came out of her time of sorrow. Simbol and Lane got together and are planning their wedding. Simbol is euphoric although she refrains from talking about any wedding plans around Kenali. Despite Kenali continuing to tell her sister that she is ok to help with her wedding plans as long as she returns the favor when Christian wakes up, Simbol still attempts to avoid wedding chatter.

Secondly, God is so amazing how he doesn't put more on you than you can bear. Kenali heard Christian going over that cliff. He yelled, "God, please help me," and she touched and agreed with him right there on the phone. And God did just that.

Julia went to the morgue; Christian went into a coma with broken bones but no brain damage. The doctors call

❧ | ❧

him a miracle. Kenali receives it in Jesus' name. Every day when she enters his room she glances at her engagement ring before quoting 3rd John 2 believing that soon he will wake up to sweep her off her feet. Then she rambles on about all the happenings around town just as if he were conscious.

Oh and the third thing; even though she lost her mom, in three months she will become one to figure out the pain of childbearing. It is like her mama said, even in this, you have to take the good with the bad and count it all joy.

"Eve, girl, we gotta talk when I get to Heaven."

Kenali rubbed her rounded stomach that is full of a little fruit, which is a product of his parents' one forbidden night in an oasis shedding the pain of a love that refused to die.

About the Author

Kimberley M. Byrd is a native of Alabama where she happily lives with her husband LeCurtis.

Forbidden Fruit is her freshman novel. It is the beginning of the series of three novels followed by *Son of the Forgiven* and *Vengeance Is Mine*. She also indulges in her first love, poetry by both writing and performing it. Kimberley is the founder of Poets' Square, an outdoor poetry event designed to showcase the talents of local poets.

Her most favorite thing to do outside of smiling is to motivate others. *10 Commandments for Dream Chasers: Dream Like God is Cheering for You* is her first non-fiction, which does just that. Developing the M.O.M. (Minister of Motivation) brand is her passion in which she breathes out motivation via different channels mostly with a minute of motivation, sixty seconds of life changing videos.

To keep up with her work visit her website at:
www.WriteOnKim.com